DESS PERKINS

WARRIOR

This book is an original idea written by Dess Perkins.

Written and created by: Dess Perkins

ISBN-13: 978-1-7368532-0-7

Editor, Cover Design, and Interior Layout Design:

KennedeeDevoe/Devoe Publications

Published by: Phoenix Rising

ACKNOWLEDGMENTS

I would first like to take the time to acknowledge my courage, faith, resilience, strength, and wisdom to begin and finish my first of many books.

I would like to thank my five children and family for seeing me through this process because they were so tired of me putting them out the house, asking them questions, asking their opinions, and in their words, "being mean to them". I love you all to the end of me and beyond.

I would like to thank the Grant Family (Thomas Sr., Thomas Jr., and Erica) for allowing me to speak about their beloved mother and cherished wife, Mrs. Linda Grant.

I would like to thank my close friends and those that have turned into family, who have known my struggles and many sleepless nights. I truly appreciate you all and you know who you are.

I would like to thank Author Kennedee Devoe for pushing (bullying) me to stay on track, not procrastinate, and providing me with essential elements to complete this journey.

I would LOVE to thank those who prayed and wished that I did not make it, who thought that life and situations would break me, but I'm still here and still becoming that Phoenix (I Rise).

Last but not least, I would like to thank that special person in my life that continues to encourage me and tell me that "the person that challenges you and holds you accountable loves you more than the person that watches you stay the same and settle for mediocrity" and "There's no such thing as a bad day, only challenging moments within the day." Thank you, David.

CHAPTER 1

How It Began

There's a saying that goes, "Here's to strong women. May we know them; may we be them; may we raise them." When they created this saying, they definitely must've had me in mind. No one asks to come into this world, but we definitely have to make the best of our circumstances. The strength that I would need later on in life was embedded in me by Grandmother Olivia, who was a very strong woman and who was raised by an even stronger woman, which was my great-grandmother Cecilia Hunter. She was French Creole from Louisiana. Although they later migrated to California, my grandmother Olivia was actually born on a reservation.

I often thought of my grandmother as being a strong woman because she did whatever it took to ensure that her children were fed, clothed, and sheltered no matter what. It was always said that my grandmother and her kids looked rich. However, no one knew that during the weekends, my grandmother would drive all the way to Beverly Hills and go to rich white folks' rummage sales. She would come back with the finest pieces of clothing, and some were even name brand. The only people that knew the clothes were gently used were the people that sold them.

Grandma Olivia was a beautiful woman. She stood 5′9″ with a slender build. She had a beautiful nutmeg complexion and wore her hair in a hairstyle they called a poodle. She was a strict Christian woman that had been raised in church at the Calvary Temple on Broadway in Los Angeles, California. She would later instill her Christian values into her daughters. The girls could not wear shorts or pants until they were at the age of 13 and they couldn't wear two-piece swimsuits until they were 16. Still to this day, my family jokes and remembers that one thing about her. My grandmother would take Scriptures from the Bible, write them on a piece of paper, and then put them in this clear box, and each one of her kids would have to pick a Scripture out of it. That's the Scripture they had to say during meals, if they were praying, or anything that had to do with the church. Those were the Scriptures that they said.

Although my grandmother was married, she was a hard worker, and she was a provider for her family. She opened a restaurant called Olivia's Café. At the time, it was located near the ABC market off of 54thand 57th Avenue on Crenshaw Boulevard. Many of the neighborhood kids would come there after school to patronize her. I was told that she fed anyone that walked through her doors, and no one was a stranger. When my grandmother's kids would get out of school, they would have to go to the restaurant because she was the only worker there. They would go to the restaurant to peel potatoes, mop, sweep, serve the customers, and run the cash register. They did everything in the restaurant like a full-service restaurant would have, but it was just her and her children running it.

On the weekends, she would vend at the swap meets with clothing she had brought from Mexico. My grandma also worked for a jewelry store owned by a Jewish man they called Mr. Jay. She was his bookkeeper and housekeeper. Mr. Jay invited her into what is called the Eastern Star Masons, which is a secret society that you had to be invited to, voted into, and then approved to get in. Then they provided an Eastern Star ring as proof of membership. I was told he really liked my grandma and he made sure she was okay because she made sure he was okay as far as his books. My grandmother was doing so well that she moved the family onto Slater off of Imperial.

Although my grandmother was working hard on creating a better life for her family, somehow her children found ways to get themselves into trouble. One time my Aunt Penelope and Uncle Clyde were out, and he decided it was a good idea to steal 35 cents from a girl. They ended up going to juvenile hall. Aunt Penelope wouldn't rat him out when the police came, so they both went to juvenile hall. An officer from juvenile hall called my grandma and told her that they were in there, and she told them to keep them there all day because she was at work at the restaurant. My uncle was in total shock when my grandmother didn't scurry down to pick him up. I wasn't surprised to hear that story. After all, she was a strict Christian woman.

I was told shortly after the juvenile hall incident that my grandmother and grandfather started having martial issues. My grandmother was always working and he felt she was unfit to be a wife and a mother. He divorced her and with the help of his sister, he ended up getting custody of all seven of their children - her children. The crazy part is that although my grandmother was working hard to make sure that her children had clothes on their back, food on the table, and a roof over their heads, they were still taken from her. She was a real caretaker to him as well as her children. He saw her as unfit, only to turn around and get custody and not even take care of them. He ended up taking them to this lady's house that lived in Arizona who raised pigs. He went on about his life like he didn't have a whole family to raise. Aunt Penelope said that they ate carrots all the time. They could not sit at the woman's table. They had to sit on the floor and they had to eat out of tin pans. There was a lot of mental abuse during that time. My aunt said that the woman was very cruel to them, and aunt Penelope ended up calling my grandmother to come and get them. With no hesitation, my grandmother said, "I'm on my way." My aunt got off the phone with relief and told the carrot lady that their mom was coming and the carrot lady told her, "She'll never get y'all."

But my grandma pulled up hours later into Arizona in a 1955 baby blue Chevy Bel Air. She was confronted by the carrot lady when she arrived at the house. My grandmother told her she was there to get her kids. The woman threatened her by saying that if she dared try to enter into the house, she would call the police. As my aunts and uncles listened at the front door, they could hear the argument taking place.

My grandmother yelled, "I don't care about you calling no police. By the time they get here, I will be long gone. These are my kids."

The carrot lady yelled back, "You not taking these kids! You better skedaddle off of my property."

All of a sudden, the door slammed opened and out ran all of my grandmother's kids. One of my uncles knocked the lady down and they began running to get in the car. The carrot lady started running towards the car. My grandmother hurried up and revved up the car and sped off. After all my grandfather did to get custody, do you know he never even tried to look for his kids after that?

When my grandmother returned to California, she moved onto $55^{th}$and Morgan in South Central. My grandma ended up getting a job cooking for a special needs children's school, a private school on $54^{th}$and 7^{th}Avenue, and the students ended up loving her. She also cooked on Sundays, some good ole down south home cooking, and people in the neighborhood would show up with three dollars to buy plates. After a successful sale, my grandma would always end up sitting down and taking a shot of her favorite whiskey, Chivas Regal.

My grandmother lived in the industrial area close to where the Watts Riots occurred. After the riots, there were a lot of burned buildings left standing. A lot of children used to play in or around them. My mother would play "house" with some of the neighborhood boys in the abandoned buildings. She loved her mother immensely but defied her at every chance she got. They say my mom smoked cigarettes and drank as soon as she was able to wear hot pants. They called her fast because she liked to dress provocatively and she was a bit promiscuous. She liked older men, and the older men loved her. She stayed in trouble. They say my mom was walking somewhere one day and an older man approached her. I suppose he said all the right things, because she called herself dating him. My mom told me that he bought her things and she liked it, so they had sex numerous times. She was only sixteen years old when she got pregnant with me.

Like most teenagers, my mother was afraid to tell anyone that she was pregnant, so she hid it for as long as she could until her belly started to bulge out. When her secret was finally revealed, everyone expected my grandmother to be angry. Surprisingly, my grandmother was ecstatic that she was going to be a grandmother because I was going to be her first-born granddaughter.

However, not everyone was as excited as my grandmother. My grandmother's sister in Oakland propositioned my mom and grandma to abort me for ten thousand dollars or to give me to her, because her biggest concern was that my mom was going to ruin her life by having a kid at such a young age. Of course, they declined both of her offers. My aunt cursed me in my mom's womb, calling me a bastard child. After that, my grandmother stopped speaking to her for a while. Since I was the first granddaughter, they agreed to give me the first initial of my grandmother's name. I was told my mom did a lot of drugs while she was pregnant with me, so much that people expected me to be born with a red devil attached to my forehead. Despite my mother doing drugs, she had a healthy pregnancy with me.

On January 27th, my mother's water broke while she was sitting in the house watching TV. She frantically called my grandmother. My grandmother hurried up and got my mom in the car and rushed her to the hospital. After several hours of hard labor, I was born Oya on January 28, 1972 at 4:04a.m., weighing 7 pounds, 7 ounces, and they said all of my family came down to see my mother and me. Everyone was excited that I was born and healthy. Everyone asked why I was named Oya. My grandmother said it is an African Orisha which means a warrior-queen, one of the most powerful African goddesses. Much of her power was rooted in the natural world. She is the goddess of thunder, lightning, tornadoes, wind, rainstorms, and hurricanes. A fire goddess, she brings rapid change and aids those who seek her in both inner and outer transformation.

Shortly after I was born, my grandmother and the family moved out of Los Angeles to Bakersfield, CA. My grandma made this decision based on her heart. While residing in Los Angeles, she had met a man that swept her off her feet. Unfortunately, Mr. James didn't want to marry her. She was so distraught that Mr. James didn't want to have a real commitment with her that she uprooted her family and moved 110 miles outside of L.A. I guess the heartache was too much for her because this God-fearing woman found solace in drinking and smoking weed. Then she completely stopped going to church. Everyone was so shocked by her behavior, as she had always been a "sanctified" woman. I guess you can say that after my grandmother started to lose her way in life that things started spiraling.

Unfortunately, I don't have very many fond memories of growing up in Bakersfield. I remember one day outside playing cowboys and Indians in my grandmother's yard. There were three of us grandkids during that time. I remember playing cowboys and Indians and I was tied to a tree. I remember being attacked by red ants and just screaming at the top of my lungs, and I remember everyone rushing out of the house to see what was going on. They saw the ants all over me. They were in my hair. They were just everywhere. My aunts and grandmother grabbed me and put a blanket around me and rushed me into the house. One of my aunts was already in the house with water going in the bathtub and they threw me in the bath. They were getting all the ants off of me. I remember my grandmother being there concerned and she was saying, "Help her." I thought that was a horrific experience.

One day my mom was teaching me how to iron at an age where I shouldn't have been anywhere near something like that. I was ironing and then some type of way the iron got on top of my hand -my left hand. I screamed and my grandmother rushed in there. She got the iron off and rushed me into the bathroom and started running cold water over my hand, but nothing was helping. The burn ended up swelling up really bad and I remember all my aunts getting needles and burning the tips of them to get the pus out. I guess nobody ever took me to the damn hospital, which is crazy. I still have the mark on my hand to this day.

Things were a little tight, so we ended up moving in with this lady named Ethel. No one trusted her, but since we didn't have anywhere else to stay, everyone just tried to make it work. We all stayed in one room. Since no one trusted her, we would take turns sleeping by the door so she couldn't get in. She would always walk around the house with a frown on her face. We would be outside playing and she would just appear out of nowhere, just staring at us. She was so weird and mean. I hated living there.

Just when I thought things couldn't get any worse, they did. One day my grandma said she was leaving to go to the store. Turns out she was actually going to get ten thousand dollars out of the bank and when she stepped back in the front yard, her niece and this unidentified woman came running into the yard. The niece was yelling, "Aunt Olivia, please help me, please help me!"Her face was red and swollen.

My grandmother rushed over to her to see what was going on. She started hugging the niece, saying, "What happened? What happened?"

The niece started sobbing, saying her boyfriend had pistol whipped her.

My grandma said, "I need to go in the house and put this money up."

The niece said, "No, we have to go now before he gets away."

Reluctantly, my grandma just said, "Come on; let's go."

The niece and the woman followed her down the street. When they got down the street, they found this young man. She told him that he needed to keep his hands off of her niece. From what I was told, an argument erupted and he pulled out a pistol and shot her in the head at point-blank range. Everyone fled the scene, including the niece and the unidentified woman.

I was playing outside and heard the phone ring, and all of a sudden, I heard my mother yell, "No!"

I ran inside to see what happened. She was just sitting there crying uncontrollably. I asked her why she was crying. She picked me up and started hugging me, telling me that a neighbor had just called to say my grandmother had been shot and killed. My mother had to call her siblings and when they arrived, they ran down to the scene of the crime to identify my grandmother's body. My mother was devastated by Grandmother Olivia's death. For days, nobody was the same and wouldn't be thereafter.

A few days later, a detective came to the house. The detective interviewed everyone in the house to see what exactly happened prior to the shooting. Everyone told the same scenario to the detective, however, no one knew what had really happened after she had left the house that day. We only knew that the detective had interviewed eyewitnesses at the scene that gave them bits and pieces of the story. Unfortunately, the only person that really knew what transpired that day was my grandmother, my grandmother's niece, the niece's boyfriend, and the unidentified woman. Although they did end up arresting him and he went to trial, he ended up getting off because the niece lied on the stand and said that my grandma was interfering with their lives, had threatened them, and he was fearful, so he shot her. To top off everything, the $10,000 that my grandmother had with her that day was never recovered. We could only assume that the one of the parties stole the money.

I was distraught by my grandmother's death. She was absolutely amazing and I loved her. She was a good woman. She loved me. I remember always being up under her. I remember hugging on her legs. I remember her feeding me from her plate all the time. I know that I felt the love from her. I know that she loved me. That's what I remember about her. My mother lived in the same house, but my relationship with my grandmother was so special. It was like she was my mother. It was a loss that I would never get over.

CHAPTER 2

House of Horrors

After my grandmother got killed, my mom didn't have a reason to stay in Watsonville anymore and she didn't really have anything. She moved in with my Aunt Penelope. My Aunt Penelope at that time had just recently moved to San Francisco. I didn't like it there much because the city had a bunch of hills and I was always having to walk up and down hills. My Aunt Penelope lived at the top of this whole apartment complex and the elevator did not work. We would climb and climb and climb to get to her apartment. It was much easier going down than going up, especially with groceries. I remember I went to kindergarten in San Francisco. What I remember about San Francisco is that there were a lot of hills. You had to go down the hill to go to the grocery store and you had to walk back up the hill with all the groceries. During this time, my mother got pregnant with her second child. She named her Mindy. My mother never knew her father because she was turning tricks.

Even with the move, my mom didn't really have anything and she didn't know how to move on from her mom's death. We didn't stay in San Francisco long because I don't think my mom liked being told what to do by my Aunt Penelope. You were going to abide by Aunt Penelope's rules. You couldn't have any shoes on when you walked in her house. You had to take them shoes off. You had to always greet her when you walked in the house. Even if you'd been in the house all day, if you were out at the store, you still had to greet her when you walked back in because it's only polite to say hello to someone when you walk in their home at all times.

Having a second child while living with Aunt Penelope definitely added fuel to the fire. I heard my mom and Aunt Penelope get in an argument once. My Aunt Penelope said, "You have the nerve to have another baby here when you can barely take care of yourself and Oya. You walk in this house and act like you own it. You don't even speak when you come up in my house."

My mom said, "Look, you have way too many rules."

My aunt was yelling, saying, "This is my house and my rules and if you don't like it, you and your kids are free to go."

My mom said, "Say no more." Within a week, we were packed and moved and headed back to Los Angeles.

We moved to 59th Street. I went to 59th Street elementary school off of 2nd Avenue. I would walk three blocks to get to the school. I hated that school. I was bullied on a constant basis. There were three particular girls who always made fun of me. They always hit me, and they always had the other kids not talk to me. I remember there was no reason for it; they just did it. I don't know if it was because I was the new girl or what. They just did not like me. The girl that would bully me wasn't a real light-skinned girl but she was lighter than me and had pretty silky black hair as opposed to my coarse hair. I remember because I wanted her hair. She did not like me at all. It was like she was trying to turn the whole school against me. I remember we had to line up on the field when the bell rang in the morning and they would walk us to the cafeteria to eat breakfast. Then we would have to walk to the building and walk up some flights of stairs to get to our classroom. The teacher would always walk in front, never behind us, and that girl would hit me going up those stairs, would pop me in my head, would laugh at me, and would try to trip me. She just hated my guts for no reason.

I finally got tired of it after a while and I told the teacher that a few girls were messing with me. The teacher asked who and so I pointed them out. I remember pointing to them and she was like, "Messing with you how?"

I said, "Messing with me. They won't leave me alone and they keep picking on me."

That teacher told me, "If you can't explain what 'messing with' is, I can't do nothing about it. Go sit down."

And I never ever said anything else about being picked on after that day. The bullying never ceased, unfortunately.

I was not enjoying our new move at all. My mom said that she had a surprise for me. I was so excited since I was having such a rough time at school. My mom decided that it was time for me to meet my dad. She had gotten in touch with him some type of way. When I heard the doorbell, I was so excited. My mom opened the door. I was so anxious to see what he looked like.

As the door opened, there stood a tall man with a little bitty beard. He stepped in the living room and just looked at me. I was so excited, but then he looked at me and he said, "She looks just like my other kids. She has the light brown eyes and everything."

I had a huge grin on my face, as this was confirmation that he was most certainly my dad.

He turned to my mom and said, "But because you denied it for so long, I believed this wasn't my child. So, she's your daughter, not mine." He turned and walked out the door.

My mom just stood there in shock. I was so confused that he said I looked like his other kids, but wasn't his kid. I was terribly hurt. I cried for days. I was like, I don't have a dad. I wanted to be accepted by him so badly. I never saw him after that.

I am not sure what my mom was looking to gain from my dad and me finally meeting. Whatever it was surely didn't work. Neither was the move to L.A. for us, so we moved back to Bakersfield. Looking back, now I see we were unstable as hell. We ended up moving in with another aunt. We lived there for a while, then my mom started disappearing. Every now and then, two to three times a week, she would disappear in the evening. I remember overhearing my mom and Aunt Dee talking. My mom had met some man by the name of Earl and she liked him and she wanted to get to know him better.

Aunt Dee said, "Well, you can get to know him, but at the end of the day, he's a man and you don't need your daughters around him. You don't know him like that. You're only getting to know him so you can go over there in the evenings. You can leave the kids here. I will watch them. Get to know him first and make sure he's on the up and up before you bring your children around him."

My mom said, "He's a good man. He goes to church and everything. He used to be in the military, but he has since retired from the military. He is a widower raising two daughters and has two grown sons. I would definitely trust him around my girls."

"Look," said Aunt Dee, "He could have a million daughters. Doesn't mean he holds himself to the same standards with other people's children that he has with his own. Now, don't be so in a rush. Just get to know him."

My sister and I didn't meet him for a very long time. However, my mom would disappear with him two to three times a week. Finally, my mom told Aunt Dee she thought it was time for us to meet him. We went over on South Brown Street to where he lived.

My mom walked in his house and said, "I'm here with the girls."

Out walked a man with a big old stomach, bald-headed, dark-skinned, and a rough-sounding voice, like scraggly.

My mom said, "Girls, this is Earl."

Mindy and I said hello.

He said, "What's your name?"

My sister said, "I'm Mindy."

He said, "Mm-hmm. And who are you?" he asked as he pointed to me.

I said, "I'm Oya."

"Oya? What an interesting name."

I said, "It means I am a warrior."

"Is that right?" he grunted."You like to fight?"

"No, sir. Warrior means you're strong."

"Are you strong?" he asked.

I said, "Yes, I am."

"Only the strong survive," he said.

My sister and I got along really well with his daughters. We started going over there once a week on the weekend or once every other week. There was no spending the night in the beginning, but eventually we would stay the night on Saturdays to go to church on Sunday. We would go back home to my auntie's house on Sunday afternoon.

Aunt Dee would ask us how our day was and how the visit was. We didn't have anything bad to say since he and his daughters were treating us and Mom well. He was really nice to my sister and me. He would cook all of us dinner on Sundays. I loved animals, so I liked that he had a chicken coop in the backyard with chickens. He had multiple dogs. He had a frog pond, which I thought was gross. And he was a hunter. I felt that I finally had a daddy because he was just that good to us.

My mom got so comfortable with him around us that she started to tell us, "This is your new dad."

So that's what we believed, that this was our new dad. I remember my Aunt Dee telling my mom she still shouldn't move too fast and everything. It took about a year, but I remember after about a year we moved in with him and his daughters Candace and Wendy, who were in their teens. He had two grown sons by the names of Dan and Dave that lived together on the street a few houses up from us. Dave was in his 20s and Dan was in his late teens. My sister Mindy and I shared a room, his two daughters shared a room, and he and my mom shared a room.

Since we moved, I had to start a new school. I started attending Bessie Owens Elementary school. Unlike 59th Street Elementary, I loved this school. I finally felt like I had a family, I was in a nice school, and everything was good. Most of the kids were friendly at this school so that was like a plus to me because nobody was picking on me, and there were some cute boys in my class. I remember we used to have to line up for lunch, and I remember chasing the boys that I liked around the building. I remember doing cartwheels in the grass because that was just what everybody was doing. All the boys who ran track would do cartwheels, so I remember I wanted to be out there doing cartwheels with the cute boys. I remember there was a black teacher and she had a black aide and they didn't play games. If the class got in trouble, everybody would have to write sentences.

I had a family, I had a good school, and everything was good. Then one day I guess I just thought I was going to be grown and I got out of school on time, but I took a detour and went down this street. In Bakersfield this street is called Lake View Avenue, but the short hood term for it is The Road. I decided to walk down The Road because it was fine during the day. It was nighttime when the hood came alive and everybody came out and hung out. I think I took an extra forty minutes to get home, and when I got home, they had already called up to the school because nobody knew where I was and I had to think fast. I told them the teacher kept me after and I thought they were just going to believe that I had to write sentences. They told the teacher the lie. I had said I had to write a thousand sentences, and she made me really write them. Then things started taking a turn for the worse.

One day I came home from school and my dad Earl said to get a piece of paper from behind the floor furnace. The house was an older house and the floor furnace was attached to it, but it was rickety. It reminded me of *Little House on the Prairie*. That's the type of furnace it was on the floor. He told me to get a piece of paper from behind the furnace and I hated, that big old rusty creaky furnace. I didn't understand why - my mom was gone with my sister Mindy. I didn't understand why nobody else got the paper. Why did he wait for me to get the paper? I brushed it off like it was nothing. I went behind there to get the paper and there was no paper, but there was a giant dead rat laying back there. I screamed and started to cry, but all he did was laugh and say, "Ha-ha, that's what you get." My dad looked at me and said, "Things are going to change around here. You're getting away with too much shit."

Consequently, this wouldn't be the last bizarre incident with him mentally torturing me. Another time he went hunting for rabbits. He brought a lot of rabbits back, and he made me watch him skin them. Then he made me skin them and he made me help him cut their bellies open. I remember some of the rabbits being pregnant.

I asked him, "Why are you making me do this?"

He told me, "You need you to know how to survive, and you are my project."

He made me watch and help him do the whole process with the rabbits: cut their necks, pull the skin, pull the fur back and peel them. I remember doing that, and I thought that was the grossest thing ever in life. Then they were still jerking, which I didn't understand because he had cut their necks. He also made me clean them and then watch him cut them up into pieces and put them away in the freezer. I had known right then that I wasn't going to eat any more meat in that house.

I remember about a week later, he took out some meat to cook. He told me it was chicken, so I was like, okay, I'm going to eat it. When I took the first bite, it tasted really good. Then, as I started eating the rest of the pieces, he started to stare at me.

He said, "Is it good?" I said yes. He started laughing hysterically.

I kept saying, "What's so funny?"

Through his laughter, he said, "That was the rabbit that you cut the week before. Don't ever fucking tell me that you're not going to eat something in this house." He sat down at the table and told me, "You better finish it. Finish all of it. I am not playing with you. I will whoop your ass if you don't."

Against my will, I went ahead and complied with his request. With tears in my eyes, I finished eating. When I was done, he walked out of the kitchen laughing. I was so sick to my stomach after I found out it was rabbit instead of chicken. I went to the bathroom and tried my best to make sure I threw up every piece of rabbit meat in my stomach. After I was done vomiting, I just sat on the bathroom floor in disbelief about how crazy this man was turning out to be.

A few weeks later, we were outside in his chicken coop. When I first moved there, I was fascinated by the chicken coup. After a few months, I began to despise the chickens because they were so wild and unruly. He told me, "You're going to learn all of this."

I didn't know what he meant by all of that, but I was sure it meant that he was about to do something else to disgust me. I went in the coop with a bowl in my hand and when I got in there, he closed the door and just watched.

"Oya, go in there and get those eggs."

I was trying to hurry up and grab the eggs because the chickens were going crazy. They were pecking at me, doing what chickens do to protect themselves. I finally had enough of the chickens attacking me and I came out before he said my time was up.

He looked in the bowl and said, "Is that it?"

I said, "Yes, I was only able to get five eggs."

"Did I tell you to come out?"

"No, you didn't, but I am not going to do that ever again."

He said, "Didn't I tell you that you better not ever tell me again what you will or won't do?"

I never told my mom about any of the incidents that occurred between Earl and me. After all, he was my new father, and I guess I was supposed to be listening to him. I never had a father figure around before so I didn't honestly know if he was just being an asshole or trying to really teach me something.

We had a frog pond in the backyard. Sometimes he would go in the back to catch a few and eat them, which I thought was gross. On this particular day, he decided it was my turn to learn how to catch a frog.

He said, "Oya, I think I want some frog legs for dinner tonight. Roll up those pants and take off your shoes and socks and get in that pond. You better catch me a good one, too."

I did as I was told. I reluctantly rolled up my pants and took off my shoes. I put one foot in the pond and those frogs started jumping all over the place. I was getting ready to take my foot out of the pond when he yelled, "Don't you dare come out that pond until you catch me one!"I looked back at him and he said, "You heard me, little girl. Get your ass back in the pond!"

I got back in the pond. I was trying to hurry up and catch a frog so I could get outta there. On my first try, I caught one. I was so disgusted because the frog felt all slimy and wet. I went to place my right foot out of the pond.

He yelled, "Nope, that ain't the right one."

"Huh?

"You heard me, girl. That's not the right one. Don't come out the pond until you have the right one for my dinner."

I got back in and caught another one and he said, "No, that's not the one, try again."

I was moving around with my hands in this water trying to catch a frog. After catching about four frogs, he finally said, "That's the one. Come on out."

I couldn't wait to get out of that water. I hurried over to him and handed him the frog.

He said, "You remember you do what I say," and then he walked away with the frog dangling from his hand.

His final act of mental torture that I remember was when he went hunting one day and came back with a baby deer, which is a fawn. He told me, "I got you this fawn for a pet and you can keep it."

I was excited that I was going to have a pet.

He said, "Stand here. I need to get him ready for you." I wasn't sure what he meant by that, but I was anxious to play with the fawn. He took the fawn hung it up in the backyard by its hind legs.

I asked, "Why are you doing that?"

He said it was to make sure the badness leaves it; you hang it up and let the badness fall out of it.

I didn't know any better, so I said, "Yes, get the badness out of him," and then I went inside.

A few hours later, I heard him calling me. "Oya, it's time to come outside. Your fawn is ready."

I ran out to the back to see the fawn still hanging upside down. I said, "Is it ready?"

He turned around and said, "Yes. It's time to get the badness out of him. He turned to the fawn, lowered it, and the next thing I saw was blood. Just that quick he had whipped out his pocketknife and slit the throat of the fawn. Blood was just squirting all over him and me. I started crying because I could hear the fawn crying for its life.

On that day I realized, in my head, that no one would ever save me. I was that fawn.

After all the blood drained out, he made me watch him skin the fur off of it. He cleaned the fur and then hung it up on the clothesline in the backyard. A few days later, he made a vest for himself. I was so disgusted with him.

I had noticed things had started getting bad between him and my mom. They had started arguing more, but they would close the door. She was jumpier around him and she didn't talk a lot. Then she started disappearing. I noticed she would just leave at different times, early in the morning or late at night. She would just leave. She wasn't there all the time when we would wake up, or she would leave while we were there. It felt like she just didn't want to be there. I felt she had lost interest in us. She would make sure she was always there on Sunday morning because she would come Saturday night to prepare us for church. On Sunday morning my little sister Mindy would be in either the living room or with the other two sisters doing something or watching TV or whatever. I was the only one ever called into the room while my mom ironed.

At first, I was just sitting on the bed with him and watching my mom iron at the foot of the bed. One day he told me to scoot back some because he was always in the bed, but he was always laying down in the bed under the covers. The next week he told me to scoot back and scoot closer to him. I did as I was told. I got a little closer, like in the middle of the bed, and he just touched my shoulder.

Time went on, and he said, "Move up closer."

At that point I was up at the pillow with him, but still not under the covers with him, and my mom was still in the room ironing as usual. This time he patted me on my back.

Then one day he told me to get under the covers. I didn't really think too much of it because my mom was in the room ironing. However, I noticed that she never ever looked up from ironing. I got under the covers with him, and he touched my thigh. But that's not all he did. He was touching my thigh, still rubbing my back, and rubbing my hair. Then I felt his hand progress to the middle of my thigh. He was rubbing the top of my thigh to the middle of my thigh. Then he pretended to accidentally brush my private part, so I wouldn't be shocked or something.

One day under the covers, he finally put his finger inside of me. I remember just lying still. I was under the covers. I was lying on the pillow and I just laid still because I didn't know what to do. I remember him moving his finger in me four or five times and then he stopped. And just as quick as it started, it was done. After he was done, he started rubbing my thigh and my back and then I was afraid to move. All I can remember is waiting for my mom to tell me to come get dressed.

Finally she yelled my name and said, "Come get dressed for church."

I remember looking up at her and hoping she would ask me something, but she didn't ask me nothing. She just looked at me and told me that she loved me. I didn't say anything. I didn't complain. I didn't do anything. I thought I had made her proud. I just didn't understand. I was the only one that was being called in there all the time. She had to know what was going on, but she didn't say anything. I never said anything. I was only about 7 or 8 years old when all of this began. I just couldn't understand why something like that was happening to me.

Anything he wanted - me, her, whatever - nobody could question him. He was like a general in that house, and I guess that had to do with him being in the military. He was very strict in the beginning - very loving, but very strict. As time went on, he had started beating on my mom. I guess during that time my mom found a way to cope with everything by using drugs again.

I remember this one time he found her doing drugs. He grabbed her by the arm, yelling, "What the fuck are you doing, you junkie?"

After that fight, his daughters Candace and Wendy came into my room while my sister and I were lying on the bed. They stood at the doorway and said, "I hate that you all ever moved here. Your mom is ruining our lives. She's a fucking drug addict." They rolled their eyes and made their way down the hall to their room.

Turns out their situation was ruined regardless because he was molesting them too. Things got even worse because after he penetrated me, he started flat out having sex with me. Then, when he wouldn't have sex with me, he would have sex with his daughters. His daughters were being molested so much that they started molesting me, too.

Everyone had left. I was at home. Candace made me suck her breasts and then Wendy made me suck her between her legs. They said it made them feel good. They said I didn't do a good job and they would show me how to do it. They would do it to me to show me how to do it to them. They showed me how to suck breasts and how to go down on a woman. They started molesting me more than he was and they would tell me if I didn't do stuff, they were going to whoop me with the belt or they were going to tell him. Every encounter was always the same way. I was sucking one's breasts and then I would go down on the other one, or vice versa. They were always there together to make sure that if I wasn't making that one happy, the other one would hit me.

One day I decided that I didn't want Candace or Wendy to touch me. They told me, "If you don't, we will just tell Dan and Doug to do it."

I asked, "What do you mean by that?"

Candace said, "Dan and Doug like to touch the same way our Dad likes to touch us and you."

"What?" I asked.

"You heard her," said Wendy.

"Why do you think our dad sends us over there so late at night?" said Candace.

That shocked the hell out of me. If Earl wasn't molesting me, it was them molesting me. My new found family was turning into a nightmare.

CHAPTER 3

Evil Earl and Dirty Dave

This nightmare would continue for years, unfortunately. They would molest me more and more because my mom just started disappearing, and she wouldn't come back for days. The more and more she was gone, the more and more I became a part of him. I was becoming one of his women, but I was in elementary school. At an early age, I kind of started becoming immune to it. What was I supposed to do? No one cared for me but Earl, and he was considered my dad. My mom wasn't around, so he's the one who took care of me. I did what he said to do, but I was scared of him too.

Things took a turn when my mom came home one day big and pregnant. I could hear her and Earl going at it. Earl said, "I know that's not my baby. Tell me, whose baby is that?"

My mom said, "Don't worry about it."

Earl said, "Don't think you're about to come up in here with another man's baby. I'm already raising two kids that ain't mine already. When you have that little bastard, don't bring him back to this house."

Even when she was around physically, she wasn't mentally there. It was like she was in LaLa Land because she was high on sherm. I guess I didn't realize how serious it was until one day we heard the neighbor yelling, "I am going to call 9-1-1!"

I ran out the house to see what was going on and there was my mother lying in the street just foaming at the mouth. I yelled at the top of my lungs to Earl. He came running out of the house. I knelt down by her side and kept shaking her and telling her to wake up. Earl dropped down to his knees and was slapping her face. She wasn't responding.

The neighbor yelled, "The ambulance is on its way!"

She was shaking and shaking uncontrollably. I sat Indian style on the ground and put her head on my lap so her head wouldn't hit the pavement. I was crying and just kept stroking her face, saying, "Mommy, please don't die on me, please!" Earl was holding her hand saying everything was going to be okay.

The ambulance finally showed up along with three police officers. The paramedics were trying to hold her hands down and they were turning her head because she was foaming. One of them had his leg over her stomach, and all I remember is I kept saying to him, "She's pregnant, she's pregnant, please don't hurt my little brother or sister, she's pregnant."

The paramedic told me, "Get back, get back, we got to handle this."

They injected her with something and then they took her away. Earl hopped in the ambulance with her. In my mind, seeing her like that as a kid, it looked like they were hurting her and I just didn't think she was going to come back. When Earl got home, he was direct and told my sister and me she had overdosed on PCP.

She didn't come home for days. I was scared. I thought, this is where I'm going to be forever with Evil Earl. She's not coming back. I was really scared that I'd never see her again.

She ended up coming home after a week, but nothing changed. Earl was still abusing me and his daughters. On top of that, when my mom came home, he was mad at her because he said that she put us in jeopardy.

I heard him say, "Do you know that you could've gotten these girls taken away from me?"

"Your girls? Those are my daughters."

He said, "They belong to me now. Your little overdose stunt could've caused me to lose custody of them."

"What? Custody? You aren't even their biological dad!" yelled my mom.

"You heard me," he said.

In retrospect, I don't think he meant in jeopardy as far as the state taking us. Maybe he meant getting taken from him because he was having sex with his daughters and me and he was worried about us getting taken from him and him no longer being able to have sex with us anymore. Either way, he wasn't worried about our well-being at all.

Shortly thereafter, my brother Marco was born. My mother didn't know who his father was either. His father was just one of her random johns. Earl stood by his words that she was not to bring that child to his house, so after my brother was born, he went to stay with Aunt Dee. Not only did she take my brother to live with Aunt Dee, she took Mindy, too. For the life of me, I couldn't understand why she would just leave me there.

I was now in sixth grade, and I started developing early. As I started developing, Earl started letting me go places, but I could never go anywhere without Wendy or Candace or Dave or Dan. I was allowed to go with Candace and Wendy and Dave to a birthday party one time. We got there during early evening, but it was nighttime before we ended up leaving because I remember it was really dark outside. I remember having a lot of fun. We were playing, there was a lot of food, and things seemed normal. I was actually having a good time for once in a long time. I was relieved that I wasn't in the house being fucked, so I thought it was a good day. I felt like things were starting to get better since Evil Earl hadn't had sex with me for at least a week, and I felt life was good.

I thought it was cool that I could attend more parties. I was going to a lot of parties with Candace, Wendy, Dave, and Dan. This one particular party I ended up having sex with Dave. I went into the bathroom, and when I came out, there was Dave at the door. He pushed me back into the bathroom and started kissing all over me. I tried to fight him off, but he told me, "If you make a sound, I will kill you." I just started crying as he threw me to the bathroom floor, pinned me down, roughly removed my pants, slid my panties to the side, and forced himself inside me. All I did was stare at the ceiling until he was done. When he was done, he grabbed some tissue and wiped himself off and told me I better not tell anyone.

"Hurry up and pull your stuff up. We got a party to get back to. And clean your face."

I did as I was told as he watched. When he opened the door, there stood Candace and Wendy. Wendy said, "See, I told you she would like it."

Wendy and Candace set me up. Earl would make them go down the street and have sex with Dave at his house. I believe they were trying to set me up because they were tired of Dave having sex with them, so now it was my turn. So now I was getting molested by the two sisters, Evil Earl, and Dirty Dave.

I never told a soul all this was happening. I was hoping that eventually it would just stop. I couldn't wait to escape the madness. I guess I wasn't the only one who felt that way because shortly after Wendy's eighteenth birthday, I remember Earl was sitting in his favorite chair and Wendy said she was going to take the trash out. However, she didn't go into the kitchen. She came out of her room with a trash bag. She went to take the trash out and nobody thought anything of it. A little bit of time passed, then a little bit more time passed, and everyone started wondering where she was. Turns out she had run away. She was eighteen. Earl had no control over her and I guess she just couldn't take it anymore.

She didn't run too far. Turns out she only ran away across the street to the neighbor Isaac's house. Isaac lived two houses down across the street. She had started dating Isaac and so she decided to run away and be with Isaac. I was actually surprised that Earl wasn't more upset - at least that's what he said. He was pissed, but not like how I thought he would be. I knew Wendy was his favorite. I remember he used to say she looked just like her mom and reminded him of her. He made it like she was destined to take care of him or something. There was nothing that Evil Earl could do but accept it because after all, she was considered an adult. Like what could he have done? Called the police? Then what? Jeopardize us by saying that he was sexually molesting us all every day?

It just seemed like things would always get worse before they got better. Earl was upset about Wendy leaving, so he was taking out his frustrations on everyone, including my mother. I heard them arguing one day from the kitchen. The next thing I heard was, "Earl, you better not!"

He said, "I'll do whatever the hell I want in my house."

I walked in the kitchen to see what was going on and I saw Earl put his hand on the top corner of the refrigerator to make it fall on my mother. She didn't have time to move, so the refrigerator ended up falling on her. He said, "I told you not to tell me what to do in my house, bitch!"

Earl looked up and saw me and said, "You better not say nothing. If you ever tell anybody anything, I will get the evil out of you."

So I didn't. I was scared of Earl. When he said get the evil out of you, all I could do was think about the deer that he killed in front of me, so that's one of the main reasons I was so scared of Earl. After I saw what he did to my mom, I was more afraid. My mom had to stay in the hospital for two or three days. During that time, Earl was really nice. He let me play outside, he let me get ice cream from the ice cream truck every day. The upside of it all was that he didn't touch me or anything for a few days. I finally was feeling like a child, and doing child things. For a small moment in time, I was finally happy. I honestly believe that was just to get my mom home and make sure nothing was being investigated.

My mom didn't come home after she was released from the hospital. She had disappeared longer than her usual spurts. When she finally came home, she looked different. She looked better. She didn't look like she was on drugs. She always had a glaze in her eyes and she used to look like she didn't care, but when she came home that day, she looked like she cared, and like she was in a good space. I had been too resentful that she had left me there with him by myself. But it was amazing seeing her looking clean and healthy. Come to find out Aunt Dee had helped her get back on her feet and was helping her find a place.

She told me, "Oya, go get your stuff. We're getting out of here."

She didn't have to tell me twice! I gathered what I could to fit into trash bags, and whatever couldn't, I just left. I was packed in less than ten minutes because I couldn't stand to be in the house with Evil Earl for another minute.

All I wanted for my mom to do was literally love me. I thought about all this bad stuff that happened, but she was there now, so I had to forgive her.

She took me to this apartment. We walked up these stairs and I remember her unlocking the door, and then she said, "We're home."

"Whose home?" I asked.

She said, "We're home. This is our apartment."

When she opened the door, I saw Aunt Dee, Marco, and Mindy in the living room. I looked at the apartment and I cried, because we had never ever had anything of our own, ever, down to our clothes. We had never had anything that was ours. Everything was either hand-me-downs or we always stayed with somebody. In that instant, I hugged my mom and I was just happy and I told her

I loved her. We didn't have any furniture, but it was our own apartment and it didn't matter. There we were, one big family, living under one roof like a normal family.

Well, normal didn't last very long because my mom started to have a lot of old white men coming over. They were wrinkly and pink. Ugh! She would take them to her bedroom, and maybe thirty minutes later, they would come out. She would always tell me, "This is Uncle such-and-such" or "this is Uncle whoever". It was a lot of uncles. But I knew my mother was turning tricks. She had started back doing drugs and that's how she was paying for it. My mom would sell all her food stamps. We would hardly have any food. We were always absent from school on the 1st and the 15th because that was the day she got the welfare check. Things weren't that great, but thank goodness we were still in that apartment and away from Evil Earl.

I was in junior high school by this time, but I didn't have many friends. There was a black couple, a husband and wife who had three daughters who lived downstairs. I could tell they had money. My mom would make us stay in the house because she would be gone for several days at a time. We couldn't answer the door, and she made sure we didn't answer that door. The three daughters downstairs would see us peeking through the window. They would wave and scream for us to come outside and play. We wouldn't dare step foot outside because we knew if our mom caught us, there would be hell to pay. Since we couldn't come outside, the three daughters would use a broom to hit their ceiling to communicate with us to let us know they were coming up the stairs. They started sneaking up the stairs to play with us and they would make sure they were looking around to make sure she was not coming around the corner or nothing. We could never go outside. We couldn't do anything and if we did go outside, we could only sit at the top of the steps. So they would have to come up to us, come up the steps to the top by our door to even interact with us. They would give us food.

I remember the oldest daughter. They all had really nice clothes. The oldest daughter would let me wear her clothes to school to make it look like I had stuff. I used to love this big old pink sweater that she had, and then she had these flower pants that had different colored flowers in them, but they had pink in them, so they matched the sweater, and then my mom had bought me these pink Pro Wings, so I had the whole hookup. That was my favorite outfit. I wore it at least once a week. I thought I was really cute in that outfit. I didn't have long hair, but I wore a feather on the left side and then the right side was braided.

The daughters and their parents really watched out for us. I believe they knew how my mom was and knew that my mom did drugs and all that kind of stuff, so they kind of took us under their wing. We needed people like them at that time in our lives because when my mom was good, she was a good mom. But when she got on them drugs, she didn't know us, she didn't care to know us, and she didn't care about us.

CHAPTER 4

CPS

One day Child Protective Services showed up on our doorstep. Of all the days they would show up, my mother wasn't home. We opened the door and they came in and saw we didn't have any furniture, and no food. They started asking us questions and we were telling them the truth.

"When was the last time you ate?"

"Like two days ago."

"When was the last time you saw your mom?"

"Two to three days ago."

"Where does your mom go?"

"We don't know."

The whole time they were there, my mom never showed up. We got taken from my mom.

After we got taken, they told her she had to do parenting classes. Took her maybe a month to complete the parenting classes and then they let us go back to her. After we got taken, you would think she would have learned her lesson. But no, she started doing the same ole things again, including selling her food stamps. We would be hungry as hell sitting up in that apartment. I decided to start stealing. That was the only way I could feed my brother and sister because in my mind, I had to take care of them. I didn't care what happened to me, but I had to take care of them. I would put on a big sweater or a skirt and some boots and I would walk to Albertsons to steal a loaf of bread. I would stick small stuff down in the boots. I would take packs of cereal out of the box and put them under my sweater. I would get lunch meat, bread, mayonnaise, potatoes, and rice. I would steal stuff that could last for days. Every couple of days after we would run out, I would go back to the store and restock up to make sure my brother and sister ate. I was a good thief. I did whatever I needed to do to survive. I was a warrior.

My mom saw how good I was at stealing, so she decided to make me start stealing for her habit. People would come to her or she would go to the dope dealer and say, "I need a 20 rock or whatever, and I don't have no money, but my daughter can go get you whatever you want." They would take me to the mall. We would go in the store, they would point out the stuff they wanted, I would get it, they would take me home, and they would give my mom the stuff - her rock cocaine.

I did that for years. During that time we probably got taken from her maybe two more times and we always went to Jamison Children's Center, which was a 24-hour Temporary Shelter Care

Facility, operated by the Human Services Department of Kern County. It was for abused, neglected, and exploited children, where children were temporarily housed who are taken into protective custody by law enforcement agencies or social workers. In addition, we were in and out of foster homes and group homes but back then, if the parent completed the parenting classes, you could go back with the parent and the kids didn't have anything to say about it. You were going back regardless if you wanted to or not.

I was getting so tired of the lifestyle that we were living. Although I was good at stealing, it was to make sure that my siblings were fed. My mother would have me steal so she could get drugs and one time, I didn't get anything. I kept saying, "I can't get it. I can't get it." The dope dealer still had to be paid, but I wanted to see my mom hurt like she always hurt us. I used to dream of ways of her to die. I wanted her to die. So I wanted him to hurt her.

I got back home and said I couldn't get anything, and that dope dealer slapped her and told her, "You going to have to get me my money."

She was so upset with me that she beat me like I actually stole something. She used an extension cord on me. I have a welt in my inner left thigh that's still there to this day from that beating that never went away. That was the day I decided I had enough and I ran away, but I ran away like five blocks because I didn't know where to go. I really didn't know nobody.

I ended up at my aunt's house. My mom was calling her and saying, "Oya ran away. Have you seen her? Has she come over there?"

My aunt lied for me. When I got to my aunt's, she was very understanding and didn't scold me. She just made dinner with some rice (without sugar…ugh), chicken, and rolls. I hadn't had a real home-cooked meal in a long time. I just thought it was the best meal in the world. To top it off, she made banana nut bread, and she was like, "If you don't try the rice, you're not going to get no banana nut bread." and she knew I loved banana nut bread.

My meal was disrupted by a knock on the door. My aunt went to see who it was. She came back in the kitchen and said go in my room and close the door. I took my plate and ran in her room. I closed the door and locked it behind me.

I could hear my mom walk in the house. "Where is Oya? Where is my child?"

My aunt said, "She isn't here. I already told you that over the phone."

"I know you're lying. I know she's somewhere in here."

My aunt asked, "Why are you making her do all this stuff? Why are you having your own daughter thieve for you? You need to just let her be a child."

"That's my child. You can't tell me nothing about her. You need to mind your own business. Now again, I am going to ask you, where is my child?" I could hear my mom's footsteps starting down the hallway to get to the bedroom door.

I was so scared because I knew she was going to kill me. I hurried up and tried to hide. I was on the side of my aunt's bed hiding. I could hear them tussling over the doorknob.

"Let me in here. I know she's in there," said my mom. I heard a stumble and bump and the door opened suddenly and there stood my mom. She said, "You think you can run from me? I am your mother. I will always find you." She grabbed me by my ear, slapped me upside my head and said, "Bitch, you going to bring your ass home right now."

My aunt came in the room and said, "Stop talking to her like that. Get your hands off that girl."

My mom said, "Mind your own business. This is not your concern. This is my daughter." She started dragging me out of the house. I had on a skort with belt loops. She grabbed the back of the skort and gave me a wedgie. I walked all the way home like that all while she was hitting me, going down the street for five blocks till we got back to the house. When we finally made it home, she beat my ass. Unfortunately, my attempt to flee was short-lived and I was back to stealing for her. I didn't want problems from her, so I made sure I got everything that was asked for.

I just really wanted to have a normal childhood and definitely knew this wasn't it. I struggled socially in junior high. I just wanted to be included. So when this boy in my class took notice of me, I was excited. He was brown-skinned with green eyes. His eyes were so beautiful and he looked like a cat. I was in love with him. And he noticed me. I thought he really liked me. I was thinking to myself that somebody finally liked me for me.

We had been going out for a while and one day he told me, "We have been talking for a little bit and I want you to come over. My mom ain't home."

Of course, I knew what that meant, so I told him, "Cool." This was going to be my first time willingly having sex with someone.

We left school and went down the street to his house. When we got to his house, he told me that I would have to come through the backyard because he tried to say his mom might be in the living room. He said I would have to climb through the window. I wanted to see him so bad so I came around and climbed through the window. I had a skirt on, but I did as he said. As soon as I came through the window, he told me lay down on the bed. I laid down on his bed and I pulled my skirt up and I pulled my panties down. As soon as I did that, all his friends came from under the bed and they started taking pictures of me.

I was so embarrassed. I hurried up and pulled up my panties and lowered my skirt down. I busted out of his room and ran right out the front door. I started walking home. I looked back and

I saw him and his goofy friends following me. They started taunting me, calling me a slut and hoe. Then some girl came out of nowhere. She turned out to be his girlfriend. She approached me and said, "Bitch, he didn't want you anyway. He just wanted to make fun of you. You're a toss-up."

I felt like crying right then and there, but I wasn't going to dare give them that satisfaction. They didn't let up off of me until I got maybe a block away from my house. A few days later, he ended up asking for forgiveness and I forgave him.

I was just hoping that life would get better but instead, I began getting bullied by this girl. She didn't like me, and there was not even a reason not to like me. She just didn't like me, and I was scared to fight. When we would get out of school, she would follow me home because we sort of took the same way home, and every day she would hit me. I was scared of her because she could fight. I was not going to fight her back no matter what she did because I had seen her fight and she even beat boys up.

One day while walking home, she hit me in the back of my head and I started crying and telling her, "Stop. Just leave me alone. Why are you messing with me?"

She hit me again, and I started running. She hit me again from behind. I never ever turned around to hit her back because I was that scared. I had been bullied all my life, and all it made me think about was the girls in L.A. who bullied me in elementary school.

The next day she just was telling the whole school she was just tired of messing with me and she was going to beat my ass at the park. I was petrified, but I didn't have a choice. Everything came to fruition after school at the park. She was waiting for me to pass by. I thought if I didn't utter a word, everything would be fine. Nope! She saw me, walked up to me, and started beating the brakes off of me. She beat the shit out of me. I walked home bloody. When I got home, my mom wasn't there, but my brother and sister were there. They didn't know what to do because I was the oldest.

The next day I passed her in the hall at school. I had some Now and Laters. She said, "What kind of Now and Laters are those?"

"Watermelon."

She asked, "Can I have some?"

I gave her two and she didn't mess with me no more after that. What the entire hell! Shit, I could have given her some Now and Laters way before if I would've known that would save me from an ass beating. I never told my mom what happened. Not quite sure why. Probably because she would've beat me and the girl's ass.

My mom ended up getting arrested maybe a month or two later. She got arrested for prostitution. I know she was doing a lot of that along with drugs. My Uncle Jay had to come take care of us while she served her time. She was going to be locked up for about three to four months. She didn't want to stop getting her welfare check or stop getting her food stamps, and she didn't want us going to Jamison. Going back to Jamison would definitely stop her welfare.

My uncle slept in the living room. I slept in my mom's room because he wanted me separate from my siblings. He started letting me go out because he said that I was older and I needed to get some freedom. He would let me go hang out with my friends and I thought it was because I was the oldest. The first few days were okay, but then my uncle would start rubbing on my back and legs nightly. Consequently, I knew what that was leading up to. I didn't know what to do so I started drinking. I drank every night. I drank until I would pass out. I drank so I wouldn't know anything or be coherent. I just literally drank, and I drank everything. I would down a 40 ounce for the hood because I loved the hood. I would drink Mad Dog and Cisco. I remember drinking Night Train with Kool-Aid and gin and juice. It didn't matter in what order and it didn't matter if I was mixing it. I knew I always had to go home to deal with what my uncle had told me I would be coming home to - have sex with him or him feel on me –so I had to prepare myself some kind of way.

One night I came home and he told me if I didn't let him fuck me, he would start messing with my siblings because I was coming of age, and he wanted to teach me how to handle myself as a woman. But I wasn't a woman. I was drunk, scared, and silent because I thought I had to save my family. It was my duty to protect my siblings. I didn't care about myself. I had been used all my life. No one ever protected me.

I remember the first time I had sex with him. He was rough. I literally felt everything until I didn't. He didn't use a condom; he just had sex with me. He hurt me and I was bleeding, but I never made a sound. He told me I better not make a sound because he didn't want my brothers and sisters to hear nothing. I would just lay there.

We had sex every single night. One night I just felt like I couldn't because my body was so tired. I was tired. So I locked the bedroom door, which wasn't allowed. I remember my body felt completely used up. My insides were tired, my outside was tired, and in that moment, I couldn't protect nobody. I couldn't protect myself, I couldn't protect my siblings, so I locked the door. I don't know if he messed with them or not, but I just couldn't. I couldn't.

The next morning when I finally came out the room, he slapped me and told me I better not ever lock the door again. I left to go to school, and when I came home, the door no longer had a knob on it. I could never lock it again.

My Uncle Jay had sex with me every night for the duration of my mom's jail sentence. I stopped going to school. He didn't care that I was his niece. He didn't care that I was a kid. The way he was having sex with me, I was just a piece of meat, and he was huge.

Lord, I was so glad when my mom finally came home and he didn't have to be there anymore. I guess things were back to normal - well, whatever normal was for us. She still did her drugs, but at least he wasn't there.

The next big thing that was coming up was my eighth grade graduation. Eighth grade was cool. They did everything on campus. The eighth grade dance would last 30 or 45 minutes of the regular school day. There were so many activities for us, like eighth grade breakfast and lunch.

A gang, Westside Crips, had been trying to recruit me since seventh grade. They would be across the street at the park, selling drugs. I finally decided to see what they were talking about. They said they were offering protection and nobody was going to mess with me if I was with them. They said, "We have to jump you in. You have to fight us. If you don't fight us, you can't join."

I wanted to have the protection because I knew if anyone messed with me, they had to mess with them too. They jumped me in after school one day. They didn't make me sell drugs, but I held them sometimes. I was now considered an active gang member.

The decisions that I was making were reckless, but I didn't know any better. I just wanted to escape from this terrible life I was living. I thought life was getting a little better for me, especially when the eighth grade graduation trip to Magic Mountain rolled around. I had never ever been anywhere so I wanted to go so bad. It was $40 and it paid for your entrance and your lunch. We were going to go on a Saturday, leaving at 8 a.m., and then we would get back it said at 5:00p.m. This trip would finally be my escape from the chaos in my life.

My mom had paid the $40 a few weeks prior. For once, she actually thought about me instead of thinking about herself. She said, "You need to go. It's your eighth grade graduation. You're graduating."

I was excited. I was trying to get okay grades because you had to have at least C's to go. I had missed a lot of school, and it always felt like I was walking into the belly of the beast every night, every day, because I never knew what to expect when I got home. I didn't know if I would be beat, molested, or treated like an errand boy/thief for my mom.

I was excited that my mom spent forty dollars on me - until the day of the trip. I got up to get dressed and she told me I wasn't going. And I was like, "What do you mean I'm not going? I already paid."

"I need that forty dollars. I owe such and such. And I got to give him his money."

I started crying."Why would you do this? Why would you do this? It's my eighth grade graduation. We're going to Magic Mountain."

She slapped me. She said, "We going up to that school, and we going to get my money back."

When we got to the school, she went straight up to the principal and told him she wanted her money back, even though there was supposed to be a no refund policy. I thought I still had a chance because there weren't supposed to be any refunds. Deep down inside I was hoping that she would change her mind because it was non-refundable.

When the principal said, "Sorry ma'am, no refunds", she went completely off. When I say she cussed everybody out, I mean everybody, including the bus driver, and he didn't even have nothing to do with it. Hell, she even started cursing out the kids. She didn't care. I don't know if she was high that day or not, but she didn't give a damn. I was so ashamed all I could do was put my head down as everyone in earshot was looking at both of us like we were crazy. Other parents started complaining about how irate she was.

They finally gave her money back because it was getting later and later for the bus to leave. I watched all the kids get on the bus and to go on the trip. I saw all the joy and the smiles on everybody's faces. As we walked home, I had tears in my eyes because she knew I was excited about this trip, but she didn't care. It was supposed to be for my accomplishments and she didn't care. As I started crying, she told me to shut up and hit me upside my head multiple times as we walked back home. She told me multiple times, "Shut up, bitch!" Those were the words that always left her mouth though. We were never called by our names. We were always "motherfuckers" and "bitches". And that day wasn't any exception.

When she got home, she paid for drugs, of course. All I could think was, *You love your drugs, you love these dope dealers, you love everybody more than me, more than us. Why are we here?* I thought about suicide. I never would go through with it, but I thought about it, especially on this day. I thought about ways to kill her. I thought about ways to have her killed. I remember dreaming I wanted her to walk across that busy street and have a bus hit her. I thought about stabbing her in her sleep. Life would be better without her, because life was hell.

There weren't many happy moments as a kid. We never, ever had birthdays. We were never celebrated. I don't remember her ever even saying happy birthday. I don't remember her ever saying she loved us - ever. She never hugged us. I feel like we were just objects there to get her welfare and her food stamps, and that's all we were. We were a means to an end and we didn't mean anything.

During my junior high years, there were a lot of men who came in and out. Then Evil Earl came back into the picture. We didn't even know she was having communication with Earl. But Earl had a camper, and Earl wanted to pay me $15 to clean his camper. He would drive his camper and park it in front of our apartment building and my mama would make me go out there and clean his camper. But he really wanted me out there to have sex with him. I would have to "clean" his camper once a week or sometimes twice a week; just depending on if he "messed" it up. For a good year this continued until Evil Earl stopped coming around. Within that year I didn't get to keep a red cent of any of these $15 transactions. I had to give it to her. Unfortunately, this wouldn't be her last time "pimping me out".

Wendy ended up marrying Isaac after she ran away. I guess things weren't working out for them because all of a sudden, I started seeing him over at our apartment. Him and my mom reconnected some kind of way. I couldn't even tell you where that came from, how it came about, anything, but then he started coming over and they were having an affair. My mom was having sex with Isaac. I remember Isaac would spend the night. In the middle of the night after he and my mom would do whatever it was, whatever they were doing, he would crawl - no lie - crawl down the hall like a creeper and sneak into my room. We couldn't sleep with our doors closed because my mom didn't allow it and he would come into my room and he would finger me and mess with me and eventually he started having sex with me. So he was having sex with both my mom and me.

To add more craziness to the equation, my Uncle Jay started visiting my mom. By this time, my Uncle Jay was doing drugs too. One night Isaac, Uncle Jay, and my mom were at the house and they were all doing drugs. My mom had called me in the living room where they were all sitting. She said, "Here, come hit this." She handed me a lit cigarette. I did as she said. I took a puff and almost coughed up a lung. She said, "Here, take this."

I said, "What is this?"

She said, "It will make your pussy hair grow."

I said, "No thank you."

She said, "Girl, just drink it. It's gin and juice. Now drink up."

I drank all of it in one gulp. I was so tipsy I would come to and then I would be out. My mom got so high she ended up passing out. Once she passed out, I walked down the hall holding the wall, trying not to pass out myself. I could hear Uncle Jay saying, "Where you think you're going?"

I just ignored him and kept walking to my mom's room. I was on my mom's bed when both Isaac and Uncle Jay came into the room. Isaac came and sat down next to me with a drink. "Here, have some more," he said. I said no and pushed the drink away.

Uncle Jay said, "Don't be rude. He offered you a drink. Drink up now!"

I took the drink and swallowed it quickly. I felt woozy. I couldn't feel my body. All of a sudden Isaac and Uncle Jay both had their hands in my pants and they were feeling on me. I couldn't fight the wooziness any longer. The last thing I remember was them feeling on me and then seeing black. All I know is the next morning when I woke up, I was sore. I felt so disgusted the next day that my own mom allowed this to happen to me. I was really starting to get fed up and I was losing the fight in me.

Sometimes I just wished I was in foster care or a group home because life couldn't be any worse there. I just wanted to get away. I was so lost. I thought my dreams were coming true one day when the neighbor downstairs saw a bunch of shadows passing her window and she yelled out, "Raid!" There were some other dope dealers over there.

Everybody started scurrying. You could hear the boom as the police used a ram to bust in doors. You could hear everyone going into the bathroom trying to flush everything. You could see the drug dealers outside that got caught trying to run with guns to their heads.

Then they came upstairs and hit our door which was illegal, because they only had a warrant to hit the downstairs apartment, but they tried to say they thought it was one apartment. They had probable cause to go into our house as well, even though they didn't have the warrant for our house. My siblings were in their rooms crying. I was sitting in the living room and they were asking me questions. All I was doing was watching as they were tearing up the little bit of stuff that we had. They ripped stuff up. They were on a mission to destroy. They ended up arresting four people from the complex, but not my mom because they didn't find anything.

After the raid was over, it was time for the cleanup, which took days and being that my mom's nerves were so bad from the raid, I knew what was coming next. One day I remember my mom told me I needed to go take a bath and I needed to smell good, because she was taking me somewhere. I did as I was told. She walked me down to the 7-Eleven and there was a dope dealer who had just gotten out of jail. She told him do whatever it was that he needed to do. He smiled and handed her a 50 pop.

My mom made me have sex with him sometimes. She pimped me out to him regularly. That was the first time me and him had sex, but it continued weekly. I started drinking more and more and more. I didn't care where I drank, how much I drank, or what happened if I drank. I just wanted to get wasted. I didn't care what happened to me.

Evidently, he wasn't giving her enough money or drugs because she started selling me to other men. I became a sex slave to my mom and her random white men.

CHAPTER 5

So Many Uncles

I went from turning tricks here and there for my mother into it happening on a consistent basis. My mother slid it in so slick on me. All of a sudden, I had a lot of uncles that were white men. I used to always think, how are they my uncles? And they not the same color as me. They're old, they're ugly, and they're white. But come to find out, they were my mom's johns.

One day she told me I was coming of age and I needed to earn my keep. At first, I didn't know what she meant by that. I was like, earn my keep? You know, I'm just a kid. How am I earning my keep? I didn't understand that. I didn't know what she meant until one day one of my "uncles", one of the old ugly white men, came over. I would get prepared and the johns would come over. I would have to bathe, put my hair up, and put on my Exclamation perfume and red lipstick. Then I would go to the back in my mom's room, and thirty minutes later come out smiling. There were quite a few. Some regulars and then some that weren't so regular. There was one "uncle" in particular that wanted me instead of my mom. He told my mom he would give her extra. She told him to go ahead. I went in the back room with him and we had sex. Later on that evening, my mom told me I was helping the household. Every time it was time to have sex, I was "helping the household."

Every time I had to sleep with those white prunes, I would have an out of body experience. I couldn't remember going to the room, any of it. I couldn't remember taking off my clothes. I could never remember the acts. But I always remember coming to. I just knew each time I was done, I was in pain. Sometimes I would start crying and typical of my mama, she told me to shut the fuck up and go take a shower. With my mom, we didn't have names. It was always shut the fuck up. Go fucking do this. We were motherfuckers and bitches. That was our names. I literally can't remember my mom ever calling me by my name.

I was having sex so much that my body was tired and worn out. I have had more men enter my body than I can even remember. I had a lot of sex growing up - a lot of it. The johns started offering her more money, which just made everything for her better because she could buy more rock. I think the money became enticing to her because there wouldn't even be preparation for me after a while. She would just be like, "It's time." I knew that meant I was about to have sex with somebody. Didn't matter who it was as long as they gave her rock or gave her money to go get her rock. When it was time, I knew I had to either take a shower or take a bath. It was second nature.

I had sex with a lot of gang members and since I was considered from the west side, that's where she got most of her drugs. So whenever they wanted me, all we had to do was walk down the street to the corner to 7-Eleven, because that's where we met them. She didn't want them to come into the house. I don't know if it was because she didn't want the neighbors to see it. My mom would leave and that's where I would get picked up by them and when we were done handling business, that's where I would get dropped back off.

I had sex for so many years. Sex became second nature to me, and pleasing a man with sex became my first nature. I pleased and did whatever I had to do until I couldn't do it no more. I was told by multiple men that I would be nothing more than a mattress to lay on, that I was messed up and damaged goods. I literally heard that phrase seven or eight times growing up. I was promiscuous because I didn't care anymore and I started having sex just to have sex. It was to a point where I didn't even have to get paid for it. I was just having it. Okay, you want to go home with me? I'm drunk, whatever, it doesn’t matter. That phrase was part of the reason that I started literally trying to change my life later in life, because that phrase irked me so bad. I would be nothing more than a mattress for men to lay on. I hate that phrase. But it's a part of me so, you know.

All of this before I was even in high school. After a summer filled with pleasing men for sexual acts, on the first day of high school, I got into a fight. I'll never forget that fight. We were in the cafeteria. It was lunchtime. I don't even know why the girl didn't like me because I had no idea who she was. But I remember we were in a taco salad line and all the security was sitting at the table. She said something. I remember us coming out the line. And we just started fighting in the cafeteria. I don't even know why.

Unfortunately, this would be one of many fights I would have during high school. I didn't care about school or anything that it had to offer. I fought all the time. I ditched classes, I pulled the fire alarm to get everybody out of school because I wasn't going to school. I probably pulled the fire alarm in my three years of high school about twenty-five times. Yeah, I was bad as hell, I really was - till they kicked me out. They finally were like, we ain’t taking you no more. You got to go. I was suspended a lot. While in high school, I always borrowed clothes from the downstairs neighbor Tracy because I was embarrassed. I was in high school and I didn't have nothing. My mom didn't buy us nothing. She never bought us new clothes. She never did anything because she never had any money to buy anything. I can't even say that we had hand me downs because I don't even know where they came from. But I know they weren't new, and after I finished wearing them, my sister wore them.

During high school, I watched my mom drink and do drugs and care less and less for us. We went back and forth to Jamison a couple times. She was in and out of jail all the time. She'd be gone for days and then come back. She was really strict when she was home, especially as far as cleaning. The house was literally immaculate. There was something about her eyes because she could see a damn grain of rice on the floor and then we'd have to sweep that whole damn floor all over again. She would go through the dishes and if she saw anything on them, she would dump all the dishes back and we'd have to re-wash them. We learned how to clean the hell out of the house.

She was bringing more and more men around in high school. I thought it was already bad, but in high school, it was way worse. There were men almost every day. They were only giving her $20 to $30. The $20 to $30 wasn't enough, so they would give me $30 to $40. She would combine all of that and use it and get the rock. She would do favors for the main dope dealer in the hood. She would have me do favors for them as well. The stealing clothes and having sex, for example. When I would get the clothes, we would take them back to my house. She would add it up and based on whatever half of it was, that's what she would get from the dope dealer. I don't remember liking sex after a while or having any kind of feelings about it.

I didn't know my body and I used to always wonder things, because my friends would say, "Oh, I can feel my periods getting ready to come on" or "I feel this" or "I feel that". But I didn't feel anything with my body. I was just there.

I feel that I honestly began needing sex. It got to a point where it was a requirement to feel good. It was a craving because it just was there and there were no feelings behind it. I didn't get wrapped up with nobody. I just did what I did. Needless to say, I was getting straight F's in all my classes. I was sent to study hall all the time to make up schoolwork when I was there. I didn't do schoolwork in study hall. Hell, I slept in study hall.

Then Evil Earl came back around, but this time it was different. My mom didn't let Earl touch me because he was only offering $15, and she denied him access to me because she could get more from other people. I remember her telling me, "You're worth more to me than $15." And I thought in that instance, I was worth more than $15, but I wasn't worth her love. She didn't love me. And if she did, I didn't know it. To me, I was only worth rocks. I was a means to an end.

I drank. Oh my God, I drank a lot. I drank 40 ounces, Cisco, Night Train, gin and juice, Mad Dog 2020 - and that could all be in one night, actually. I was taking sips out of all of it.

I became an alcoholic and didn't care. Nobody could tell me anything. I was extremely defiant. All I wanted to do was fight. I was gang banging. I started using sex to get what I wanted. My mom could get paid. Why couldn't I? I would meet up with the drug dealers at 7-Eleven. Then I began using them to get something to eat, an outfit, or you know, anything like that. I decided I might as well get what I could get while the getting was good. That was my outlook on life: get whatever I can get while I can get it.

I started losing weight. I was non-stop running, always going, always on The Road. I would go to The Road sometimes and get so drunk. I can literally remember sitting in a chair and slouching and then someone having to walk me wherever they had to walk me because I couldn't walk due to being drunk. I would go up there just to get drunk, just to see who was going to take me home, just to see who I was going to wake up to. My nights were blurred because I didn't care no more. I literally stopped caring for everybody. There was no reason for nobody to care for me. I was living in a blacked-out state of mind.

My junior year, there was this counselor who called me into her office. By that time I had so many fights and was always in trouble. I would get suspended or get expelled and be able to come back the next quarter or next semester or next school year. So this black lady, light skin, long pretty hair, about 5′4″,called me into her office, went over everything with me, and asked me, "What is your problem? Why are you acting like this? Why are you doing this? Why are you not passing your classes?" Just like a mom, just like somebody who actually cared.

I thought, *I don't know who this lady thinks she is, but ain't nobody scared of her.* "You know, I'm not scared of you, especially because you are as tall as me."

She told me that she cared. She didn't care that I was acting tough and that I was going to have to meet with her every single week, sometimes twice a week.

I asked her one time, "Why do you care? Why are you making me meet with you? I'm not your pity party, or whatever the case may be."

And she was just like, "You need some help. You're a bright girl; you're just not really applying yourself."

I told her, "You don't know my life. You don't know nothing about me. How do you know I am what I am? I don't need you."

But she stayed on my ass. I had never seen a counselor take that kind of interest in a student. She would buy me clothes. She would buy me female essentials. She would come into my classroom sometimes just to see what I was doing. She would do home visits though when she came, my mom wasn't there, so I couldn't open the door for her. But she would do them just to see if I was okay.

She cared. She showed she cared. And I know she did. She helped me obtain some of my high school credits. But she was honest. She said, "You're not going to graduate, so either you're going to go to a continuation school, or you're just going to do what you're going to do, basically. And she asked me, what did I want out of my life?

I told her, "I want a different situation. I want a different scenario. I want a different outcome."

Nobody ever cared. And she showed me she did. I wanted to make her proud of me. But then I got into it at school. There was some kind of race thing going on between the blacks and the Mexicans, and I wasn't no punk. All the blacks were against all the Mexicans. It felt like a movie scene because we literally had chains, bats, and knives. We met up behind the building and we were going to kick each other's asses. Why we didn't care for each other, I don't remember. But it was a whole war.

When the police came, everybody got kicked out. I had already been kicked out so many times that I literally couldn't come back. So the day all that happened, she was very disappointed in me because everyone was in the office: police, counselors, students, and parents everywhere. She just looked at me and she shook her head in disappointment. I just told her, "I had to do what I had to do. I had to do it for the set." I didn't care because I was getting kicked out and my homeboys were getting kicked out. We were all getting kicked out together. Before we left that campus, we went and pulled every fire alarm on the campus. And that was my last time on that campus.

When I went over to the continuation school, I fought a lot. I honestly feel like I had been bullied and picked on for most of my life, so I wasn't scared to fight nobody. I had a fight the first week at this new school with some girl. We were in continuation school together. We walked from the school for about three or four blocks and ran into California Park. That girl and me started fighting in that park. Some type of way, we ended up in the street and it was like a whole brawl, a whole Royal Rumble. We were fighting in the park by the sidewalk and in the street. The people who were watching were stopping traffic because we were fighting. Then we stopped because our bus came. It was a city bus. We got on the bus and started fighting on the bus. The bus driver stopped and we had to get off the bus. And then we started fighting again. That fight probably lasted for hours. We fought all day after school. Just didn't care. I remember the school called my mom because the police came, of course. The school was still responsible, so they still had to contact my mom. When my mom came and got me, she beat my ass.

Those ass beatings still didn't stop me from doing whatever I wanted to do. My mom would leave because she had to go get her drugs, and I would sneak out. I would leave the door unlocked or I would bribe one of my siblings to let me in. When I got back, I would knock on the door.

One night I snuck out with Tracy, the girl downstairs. We wanted to go out. It was a Friday. I just needed to get out of the house. We went to this club in the country called Dolly's. We were scared to get out because we were still in high school, but Dolly's is where everybody hung out at. And Dolly's wasn't even nothing major. It was literally a hole in the wall type club that probably could only fit three people on the dance floor. And then there was a long strip of like 5,6,7,8 buildings, all raggedy old little buildings, and then just dirt. You would walk back and forth just to see who was out there. That was the hangout spot. You got dressed to go and hang out at Dolly's. You would have to walk past men and women. People were outside checking other people's outfits out, who looked good, who didn't look good. It was the hot spot. It was the place to be.

So we got out for a minute and walked up and down the dirt. Then we went and got back to the car. When we went back to the car, Tracy's boyfriend got in the front seat with her and his friend got in the backseat with me. I really didn't think anything of it because I knew that was her boyfriend. They were just getting in the car. Well, the boyfriend didn't mess with her. But the friend was sort of trying to force himself on me and I was like, "I'm not interested."Tracy started telling her boyfriend to tell his friend to leave me alone. He told her shut the fuck up. Then her boyfriend got in the backseat.

I was in the middle and each one of them was on each side of me. They told her to drive to the projects. She did it even though she said she didn't want to, but he had told her, "Shut up before we get you too." I knew she couldn't help me when he told her that. I knew there was nothing she could do.

She drove to the projects, which was on the east side of town where The Road was. They were manhandling me. They were roughing me up, they were holding me down. They were hitting me. They were touching my breasts and in between my legs all while in the backseat.

Once we arrived at the projects, they told her that she needed to leave. And she did. They carried me - one carried my feet the other was carrying my hands - and they were forcing me to go and I remember trying to fight them. But one of them was like six feet tall and around 200 pounds. The other one was not far off from that. I couldn't fight them off. That night I had on these blue jeans they were my favorites. These blue jeans had two buttons on each knee and you could take the button down and a different color would show while the flap hung over. I had this white shirt on that came down to like the middle of your thigh. But then in the back, it had the opening a little bit. It was like a fishtail type of shirt. I remember they ripped it. They pulled my pants down. I kept trying to fight them. I was being hit by each one of them. One was holding my hand and they took turns climbing on top of me. They were having sex with me. I was in a lot of pain. I was hurting, but I kept fighting. All I kept thinking to myself was, *Are these niggas raping me? I'm being raped?* This is not one of the instances where I gave myself freely. It went on for a while. They didn't use condoms. Each of them had sex with me multiple times and this lasted for almost three hours. After they were finished doing what they were doing, they drove me back to Dolly's because that's where they told Tracy to wait for us.

There was blood everywhere. I had a big puddle of blood on the back of my white shirt. The first thing I thought was, *Y'all ruined my shirt.* I couldn't hide it. When we got back out to Dolly's, Tracy gave me her sweater to put around my waist because we didn't leave right away. She got out and walked with him for a while, knowing what he just did to me. She came back to the car and we drove home. When we got to the house, she gave me a shirt to change into and we threw my shirt away. I was in disbelief. *Like all these times I gave myself and I probably would have given myself to them because that's just what I was doing back then. But you took it and you fought me and you hurt me. And then you ruined my shirt.* I was devastated. I knew I couldn't get the blood out of my favorite shirt. I had always thought that that shirt was lucky when I wore it. It was my lucky white shirt. But that was the night that that shirt was cursed.

It was so crazy because after that happened. He came around and everything. I mean, he was her boyfriend. Nobody ever talked about it. I was still going out. It was just like I had to brush it off. Because he was the big-time dope dealer on the east side. She was dating the main doughboys, the west side one and the east side one. And nobody ever talked about it. I sure wasn't going to tell anybody that he did that to me because everybody loved him. I can honestly say I've never stepped in those projects after that because it always brings back memories. To make the situation even crazier, he looked out for me after that night. If people were messing with me, if niggas was trying to talk to me and being forceful, anything like that, or if I needed anything, I could go to him and ask him for stuff and he would get it. I remember going on The Road, and some dude was talking shit. I went and told him and he went and checked the dude. I couldn't even wrap my mind around why I would look at him as a protector after he raped me, but I did.

After the rape, I started to drink a lot. I tried marijuana, but it made me itch. I was good on doing weed. I just drank. Drinking was my drug of choice. I was still having sex. I was going on The Road almost every night. I was going to the clubs. I was getting in clubs that I wasn't supposed to get in. I was partying at the clubs. I was going home with men, whoever I would meet. All someone had to do was maybe buy a drink. This guy on The Road saw me one night. He told me come get in his car. I got in his car because I knew him.

He told me, "You're better than this. Why are you always up here? Why are you doing it? You're too young to be up here. You're too young to be wasting your life." But he didn't know what I was going through at home. He was one of the dough boys. He said, "You need to get off this Road. This ain't no place for you."

He drove me home. He didn't try anything with me. I remember really appreciating that. I thought okay, he cares, somebody cares yet again, but he didn't care enough. Not that we were dating or anything like that, but I found out he was dating one of Tracy's sisters. Everybody liked him. He was fine. He was light-skinned with a long thick Jheri Curl. He was stocky like he lifted weights. He had a nice body. He had a black monster truck that had music in it. Everybody loved getting in it going for rides with him. All of the neighborhood girls had a crush on him.

After that night, he was now talking to me and Tracy's sister. I would think to myself, *Why would he talk to me? She has the long hair. She's a pretty brown-skinned girl. They family got a little money. Here we are upstairs, barely got furniture, can't come outside, hair ain't like theirs for damn sure. I'm dark-skinned. What would he see in me?* That honestly was my whole thought process when it came to him. Because obviously if your Jheri Curl is longer than my hair, you got long hair. His hair was down his back. He got long hair, she got long hair…that was my thought process. *Why talk to this little black girl? You didn't really want to talk to me. You probably just wanted to have sex with me. You just want to have sex. Before you lie to me, I'll just give you what you want, because that's what I do.*

They were opening up this new club on The Road. It was owned by some brothers. Everyone knew or knew of the brothers. Everyone also knew they had sisters. These sisters came to the opening. They had on furs. I don't know if they were real furs, but they were furs nonetheless and the sisters dressed seductively. The sisters did the song "Sex Shooter" by Apollonia 6. They did the whole little performance that went with the video. Everybody went to this club that night because it was the grand opening.

Everybody was having a good time that night. That was a bomb night. I remember there was just so much going on in my life that one night of just having fun, that's all I was looking for. I got my chair and I sat to watch them perform. And I was just drinking. Guys were like, "Oh, you drink and drink." I had some of my homies with me. And they were like, "Toss it back for the set."So I drank the whole 40 for the set. I literally just tossed up and didn't stop till it was gone. I remember taking some sips of the Mad Dog. And then I remember drinking some Night Train with Kool-Aid.

I don't remember anything after that. There were a lot of police on the road that night, just driving up and down in their cars and some walking around, coming in and out of the club. By that time I was drunk and the police even knew I was drunk. And they told my friend, "Either you get her off this road now, or we're going to arrest her."

My friend and her friend started walking me to her friend's house. I remember my feet dragging. One of them had my arm around her shoulder. Once I got to the friend's house, I remember me still having one arm around my friend and the other arm around her friend. They were trying to walk me inside her house. It seemed like it took forever to get in that house. The longest walk ever.

When I got inside the house, they decided they would put me in the shower and put water on me. I started sweating, so they put more water on me. I started throwing up profusely. They sat me on the toilet. Of course I was shitting - you know, it was coming out of every hole I had. Looking back, it was probably alcohol poisoning. After I was done having a drunken moment and still sitting on the toilet, not being able to move, there were guys at the door of the bathroom. One of them was an ex. Her house was the hangout. They were trying to get in. They wanted to run a train on me that night. That's all they kept saying:"She ready? She ready?"They would have succeeded, but Tracy kept trying to fight them off and close the door. And the girl at the front of the door where they were, she was trying to fight them off.

They never got to run the train, thank God. But they did get in the bathroom and some were trying to finger me. But they didn't do anything other than finger me and it lasted for a while. I passed out. I blacked out. I don't know if anything happened or not after that. It took me a long time to come to. The next day, I had a new nickname. That wasn't pretty. They called me Shitty because they said it was everywhere. And I had to live with that name for almost a year.

I still continued to go out. I was out the next day, even after all that. I still continued to have sex. My mom still continued to have me as a sex slave. I just didn't care about nothing. What was I supposed to do? I don't know what I was supposed to do. I was just doing what I had to do to make it. I was getting through life the best way I knew how.

CHAPTER 6

A Real Bed

My senior year, I was seventeen years old. I'd had to go to continuation school, and I was so far behind. I couldn't even make up enough credit in a regular school year at a regular high school. I would have to go to an adult school to get the rest of my credits. I didn't have enough time, because I had damn near fucked off three years. I didn't experience a prom, senior breakfast, or a dance at a high school. I've never experienced any of that because we didn't have money. Moms wasn't going to buy me anything. She wasn't going to do any of that. She didn't care nothing about any of that. That was money that was out of her pocket. What she needed was for me to have sex to get her money for drugs, even throughout high school. I didn't graduate. Of course I didn't. She didn't care.

I just wanted someone to care for me, but it damn sure wasn't my mother. The act of caring for someone is so powerful that it shouldn't be estimated. It could be as easy as someone showing you fake love, but it still can be misinterpreted for something real.

One day I was up at the school and I knew I had to leave soon, so I started to walk towards the bus stop and there he was. He lived across the street in these apartments that are across from the school. He was just sitting out there and I gave him a look. There was nothing. The next day, same thing. The next day, he was like, "I keep seeing you looking at me, but you don't say anything."

I said, "You're doing the same damn thing."

"So what's up?"

I said, "What's your name?"

"Aubrey. What's your name?"

"Oya."

"Oya? What an interesting name. What does that mean?"

"It means warrior."

"Cool." He asked me if I minded if he could get them digits so he could call me sometime.

I said sure. I went in my notebook, ripped out a piece of paper, and took out a pen. I said, "Write your number down."

"You write yours down first."

I wrote it down, then passed him the paper and pen and he wrote his number down. We started talking on the phone every day, getting to know each other. I thought he was the man of my dreams. Everything was amazing. We dated for a little while.

Then one day, he asked me to meet his mom. I said okay, and so we drove up to where she lived, which was like on a hill. When we drove up, we parked up slanted. She was standing on her balcony. I never looked up. I just stayed looking down because he was still getting out of the truck and he was going to go upstairs, so I stayed with my head down because I was just waiting on him. Later on, she would say that I was looking at her crazy, but I never looked up and I had never even met her, so what did I look at crazy? Later on, I would find out he was talking to someone else as well and his moms liked her, so me coming into the picture was all bad.

We started hanging out and all that kind of stuff. At the time when I was talking to him, I ended up getting taken from my mom because something had happened with her again.

We ended up having to go to court. Mindy and I decided not to go back. We ended up getting placed in foster homes that were 15 - 20 minutes from each other. If you walk, it was probably more like 30 to 40 minutes maybe. I lived in that foster home for almost a year. They were an older couple that became like my grandparents. She was a stay-at-home mom and grandmother and he worked at Sears as a custodian. They had three of their grandkids - two girls and one boy - that lived in the house with him. My whole guard was up going into this foster home. I was like, all they want is the money. They don't care nothing about me. It's going to be like the foster homes that I've already been in.

But I was wrong. They made sure my bedding was clean. They made sure I had everything I needed. They put a phone in my room. I had never had a phone, and I had never had my own bed - a bed that actually was a bed, like you'd have the rail and the frame and the mattress. I've slept on mattresses, but I never had a bed until I went there. They took me and bought me brand new clothes and all the stuff that I would actually need for myself. They had French Provincial furniture with the plastic runners on the floor because you would walk through that living room to get to the family room where everybody actually was. They treated me like I was one of theirs. And then the grandkids started calling me sister. The husband helped me get my first job at Taco Bell. He would drop me off to and from work. He would pick me up. I was getting off at 10 -11 o'clock at night and he would be there.

Everything for once was good. Then Aubrey went to jail and I was accepting his collect calls. I didn't know collect calls cost so much. When the $300 phone bill came, they made me use my first, second, and third paycheck to pay the phone bill. That did not feel good. Thank God he wasn't in there long. It was just a couple weeks or whatever. I know now it was puppy love because we would be on the phone with each other all day and night and we would literally fall asleep on the phone with each other.

The only person in his family who liked me was his grandfather. They all felt that he loved me too much. I couldn't help that we were hooked and sprung in love with each other. He was honestly my first love. When the grandfather passed away, I had no allies in his family. Come to find out my mom had gotten her own place. She said, "You could come and stay with me if you want to."I was all grown up now, but she still wanted me to stay with her. I was over eighteen and I didn't know what to do because my foster parents told me I didn't have to leave, even though they weren't going to get any money for me. They didn't want me to go, and I appreciated that, but that also took away from them helping other foster youth the way they helped me. After all, I was their "child" so I would always be family. They wanted me to stay there, but I couldn't see Aubrey because he couldn't come over. So that's the only reason I left: because I wanted to see Aubrey.

They told me that I was family and I would always be family and always had a place at the house. I could come back anytime I wanted or needed to. I stayed in contact with them. Even though my foster parents took care of me and loved me, I still went back to my mom. I sometimes feel like when she was lucid, she wanted things to be right with us, especially because our relationship is so strained. Aubrey and I moved in with my mom. I did stay in contact with my foster parents. I would call maybe once a week or once every two weeks. I would call just to see how they were doing. One day I called and they told me that the husband had passed away. I was in shock.

My foster father's death would eat at me for a while so I put all my heart and soul into Aubrey. I would eat, sleep, and breathe him. We just wanted to hug and touch and kiss and have sex at all times - literally, all the time. Moving in with my mom and always being with Aubrey, I got pregnant within a month. My mom told me I needed to go apply for welfare. As soon as the number of days had passed where you get approved, my mom flipped on me. She told me, "You need to give me some money. You need to give me half." She was back on that money thing. And when she got back on that money thing, it was time to go.

I was pregnant and I moved out. Aubrey had asked his mom if I could move in with her because I was pregnant with her grandchild. Mind you, the other girlfriend that his mother actually liked was pregnant with her grandchild, too. Literally my son Trey and her son, Aubrey Jr., were conceived six months apart. I moved in and the situation got somewhat awkward when she started coming over with her son, and on top of that, she named him Aubrey Junior. I just had to accept it because the baby mama and his mama were friends. His mom only let me move in because I was pregnant and had nowhere to go. So that living situation was not peaches and cream at all because they would talk about me when she would come over.

His baby mama got an apartment. He moved out and moved in with her and left me with his mom while I was still pregnant and almost due. Even after I had my son, he still lived with her. He would come over and see our son. His mom helped me with my son a lot though.

I finally was able to move out and I ended up getting my own place. He came and moved with me and I got pregnant again. After a while, he started hitting me while I was pregnant. He was controlling. He didn't have a job and I was still getting welfare. I would get my welfare check and cash it. He had to be the one to hold the money so it looked like he had money and he was taking care of us. That was a requirement. And he handled everything. I didn't have a voice and pretty much better not say anything out of line.

I remember one time he had me go to Daniel's and open a jewelry account to buy his mom's some jewelry for Mother's Day. He didn't give me anything, but he had me open it to get her something. And I did it. He moved his brother in with us because he controlled everything. Mind you, we were in a loft. He moved his brother in with us after I had my twins, Jazz and JJ. The brother slept downstairs. We slept upstairs. The brother didn't do anything - I mean anything. He didn’t cook; he didn’t clean; he ate up everything and played video games all day. I couldn't say nothing, and I was the one paying the rent in our low-income apartment. He didn't pay nothing and he didn't have a job. The brother ended up living with us for a year.

We ended up moving out because we had outgrown that place. We had found this two-bedroom apartment. It was good for a while. Then Aubrey became different. Like he started having girls call the house. They would say he told them that we were just roommates. He was taking my money and buying other girls stuff. He started physically abusing me. I was so stressed out, but I was also at a point where I didn't think I deserved anything better. He had worked on my self-esteem in a major way. But I can also say that I had to have allowed that for that to go on and for it to happen. I was down to 119 pounds and miserable. He was gone all the time. He didn't want to be around me. He wasn't having sex with me. He wasn't touching me. There wasn't nothing else he wanted.

I remember he started hanging with this dude he knew. The dude's girlfriend started hanging with me because it was like a couple's thing. But they were literally cheating. We were sitting at home. They were cheating. He gave some girl my phone number. She called my house and she told me that Aubrey told her that we were just roommates. We were not together. We were just there to co-exist with our kids. He did what he wanted, all these different things. We were going back and forth on the phone. And then she handed him the phone. And I was like, "You dirty piece of shit. You got to come home sooner or later." I don't know what I expected I was going to do because I was already scared of him. But I was angry in that moment. I was going to try to figure out something.

He didn't come home for two days because he was over there. I was trying to find out where the girl lived and couldn't find out anything. I would call the girl's house. I could hear them in the background. They didn't care.

Eventually when he came home, we got into it. I hit him, and I ran in the bathroom and I locked the door. He busted the door open with one kick or something and he hit me so hard. He hit me so hard that I flew into the tub. He blackened my eye, busted my lip, and bloodied my nose with that one hit. I was about to call the police on him, but I was so naive that I believed his mom when she used to tell me she was worse than the police and to call her first. She was literally only looking out for her son and no one else. She had always told me, "Don't ever call the police, and don't include the police in your affairs. Call me; I will handle it." I called her. She came over. But it was just a ploy not to call the police because she didn't do anything and I looked like I'd been in a WWF wrestling match.

About two days later, I was so tired and so over it. Aubrey was sitting in a chair. I got a butcher knife and I stabbed him in his thigh. I wasn't holding the knife right…

CHAPTER 7

Ultimate Fighting Championship

When I stabbed him in his thigh, I wasn't holding it right. As I was stabbing him, I realized I had just sliced my own hand open. There was blood gushing everywhere. I had to rush myself to the emergency room to get stitches. There I was trying to kill him and I damn near killed myself. That should have been the first clue that I should probably cease and desist this relationship. But when you're young, you don't know that when a person shows you who they are, that's who they really are. There's no changing someone if they can't even see the flaws in their own character. I was just stuck on how things were in the beginning because our relationship was like a fairy tale, but as our relationship progressed, it ended up being like hell on earth. He would hit me constantly, cheated on me, and demeaned me. He really didn't care at all. The last six years of our relationship were absolutely horrible.

He even had horrible ideas on how to "get rich quick". At the time it sounded like a good idea, and since we were somewhat struggling, why not get on board? Everybody was doing it back then and getting away with it, but I guess that didn't make it alright. He had this brilliant idea to open up a bank account, then get the checks, go into stores and purchase items, and then take them back later for the cash. He was writing bad checks on the account. I guess all good things do come to an end because I ended up getting caught up in it with him. At that particular time, we were not together, and we were not living together.

He called me one night and asked, "Do you need anything for the house? Any kind of food or anything like that?"

I said, "Yeah, we can go to the grocery store."

He asked me to give him a list, and I began to rattle off everything. He said, "You need to just go with me."

The kids were asleep. I closed their bedroom door. The store wasn't far away, so I was thinking everything was going to be cool. We would go get this stuff and I'd be back home in no time.

But I never knew that he had been writing these checks a lot at that particular grocery store. After the clerk rang up our groceries, he handed her a check. She tried to process if through the machine a few times. Finally, she said, "You'll have to hold on. I need my manager to verify the check."

The manager walked over, took the check, and walked away. We were sitting there for at least five minutes when all of a sudden, the police showed up. They placed us under arrest for fraud. They took us to the Lerdo Pre-Trial Facility. We were placed in separate holding cells. I used the pay phone to make a collect call to my neighbor and I told her to go to my house and get the kids since I had left them alone, not realizing that the police were listening. They knew I told my neighbor go to my house, and they also went to my house. By time my neighbor got over there, the police had beat her there. Luckily, Aubrey had called his mom to go to my house, so the police ended up letting her take the kids.

We were charged with forgery. But on top of the forgery, I also got charged with child endangerment because my kids were left home by themselves. Aubrey was released that same night. I don't know if he got bailed out or what. But I can remember looking through the window as he was getting released and walking out. I was thinking to myself, *What about me? I came in here with you.* He never looked back to see where I was. He just walked out.

I was locked up for a month while he shacked up with another bitch with my kids. When I finally got out, I was young and still in love and believed the things that he said. Honestly, I feel like he kind of had my mind because I had been with him for so long. I was in love with him and I fell right back into the mess of believing in him.

Well, after I got out, he came and stayed with me. I allowed him to move back in. I had realized that he controlled me, my thoughts. I obviously didn't value myself. And yet again, I allowed a man to treat me like a mattress. I know I still stayed and it was my choice. After all, I was with him for twelve years on and off, off and on, waiting for a moment when I could technically break free of him. But it took a lot more years before that happened.

During those twelve years, his aunts despised me. His mom called CPS on me, I don't even know how many times, but it was beyond excessive. She spread rumors about me that I had venereal diseases. Her dumb ass was being so vindictive, not realizing that by saying that I had a venereal disease it meant that her son would have it, too.

I really couldn't stand the sight or smell of her. When she would come over to my apartment to visit, I would just pretend like she was invisible. I had never seen someone so hell bent on trying to tear a relationship apart. She acted like she was fucking him and he was her man.

One day she arrived at our place with a guy she knew who liked me. She made sure that they came over as well, him and his friend. Aubrey and I pulled into the parking lot. They were already there in the parking lot. We got out of the car. As soon as I got out of the car, she started talking all kinds of shit.

"You're a dirty whore. I don't know why my son even wants you. You got herpes, chlamydia, and trichomoniasis. I don't know what my son sees in you."

I told her, "Those are lies and just as bald-headed as you are. You better stop lying on me before I bust you in the lip." I turned around to look at him, thinking to myself, *Aren't you going to say something?* I told him, "I'm not going to take too much more. This is your mom."

He told his mom, "You can't keep talking to Oya like that." In that instant, is when she really hated me because he chose me over her at that moment. She was so mad you could see the fumes coming from her bald edges.

She started screaming, "You're choosing her over me? Me! You are my flesh and blood. You don't turn your back on your mother." She turned to me and said, "You made my son turn his back on me you hussy!" Then she pushed me.

That was it! I had enough. I punched her dead in the mouth just like I said I would. For an older lady, she took that first punch like a champ. She stumbled a bit, but caught her balance. She cold-cocked me in the eye. It was on after that. I threw so many punches you would think I was trying to win the Ultimate Fighting Championship. I couldn't believe that his mom and I were in the middle of a parking lot straight scrapping.

Aubrey finally broke up the fight. After he got us separated, he asked me if I was okay. I just nodded my head. He grabbed my hand and we began to walk off.

She was gasping for air, yelling, "This how you do your own mama?"

We just continued to walk away. I know she was hella pissed because he didn't leave with her. I thought it was all over. I was walking in the middle of the lot, headed upstairs. She got in her car and the crazy bitch tried to run me over. She bumped me with her front end. I was so livid that I hit the hood of her car and kicked the bumper. I said, "C'mon, you old bitch, let's go for round 2." She hurried up and threw the car in reverse, went around me, and sped out of the parking lot.

Even though Aubrey chose me in the moment, it would be a year before he or his mom talked to me again. Her crazy ass went back to calling CPS on me. She would lie and say that I didn't keep a clean house, I didn't have food, and I didn't wash my kids' clothes. But every time CPS showed up, it was actually the contrary they would see. They would look at the kids, they looked through the house, they would see all this stuff. Every time they would come out, they wouldn't find anything. It was just the point that it was happening once a week or once every two weeks. I had thirteen cases. All of them were unfounded or unsubstantiated.

Unfortunately, our relationship wasn't substantiable. There were so many bad times in the last five years of that relationship. I was at the smallest I'd ever been in my life...119 pounds. I didn't feel like I could get another man. I felt like this was it for me. So it was kind of like he controlled me, and that control and fear lasted even after we were totally done. I mean, totally over. After twelve years, I was finally over him beating and cheating on me. I ended it.

There I was, twenty-one years old, stuck raising three kids on my own, living on welfare, trying to make ends meet with no help from my sperm donor. There were a lot of hard days, months, and years raising three kids on my own. I remember I would call him when school would get ready to start every single year, asking him, "Can you just buy the socks, and the underwear for the kids?" He would say he would, and never did.

Even though he turned out to be a bum, I never stopped my kids from knowing their dad or seeing him because I knew one day when they got old enough, they would realize who he really was to them. They would worship the ground he walked on. They thought he could literally do no wrong. He would come to visit with a bag of 25 cent potato chips and they would just think that was the world. And I was sitting there struggling, for the clothes on their back, food in their bellies, and a roof over their heads. This Negro walked in with chips and he would get all the praise with that bag of chips. Chile, please!

Things were already tight, but then my mom somehow ended up going to jail for the hundredth time and my brother and sister had to come live with me because she was going to be in jail for 7-8 months this time. I was raising them along with my kids. They were in school and everything. It wasn't easy and times were even harder with the added responsibility but what could I do? They were family and I had to protect them.

When my mom got out of jail, I remember I was walking down the street one day, just overwhelmed taking care of so many kids, and she walked up. I didn't even know she was getting out. She said she was on her way to my place, coming to get her kids. That was a joke. Not only didn't she come get her kids, but she moved in with me. My house turned into a real-life Brady house. There I was, still helping everyone when I could barely help myself sometimes.

Taking care of all these kids and responsibilities were hard when you had to tote kids on the bus with you. I hated that I didn't have a car. Everywhere I went, I had to catch a ride, bus, or use my two feet to get there. I recall one day walking about six blocks from my place. I was coming from a homegirl's house because she had asked me to babysit her kids for her that night. I had my kids, and I had her kids, walking to my apartment. I had almost gotten home when this Cadillac pulled up full of dudes. It was this guy driving, and then three of his homeboys - two in the back, one in the passenger seat, and him. And he was in an old school money green Cadillac with the gold trim package. He was dark, tall, but a little stocky. He had a very cute smile.

He said, "I am from out of town, but I would like to get know you better. Can I have your number?"

I said, "Boy, are you crazy? Don't you see how many kids I'm working with? You don't know if these are all my kids. You sure you want to get to know me?" Because I think I had about six kids with me and I'm like, "Why the hell you pulling up on me?"

He said, "So are those all your kids?"

"Just these three."

He said, "Well, they are cute, just like they mama. What's Mama's name, by the way?"

"I am Oya."

"Oya? What a different name. So Oya, what's up with them digits? Can a brotha give you a call sometime or not?"

I blushed and gave in.

We talked a lot on the phone. He was telling me about himself, telling me he was from out of town. But come to find out he really wasn't. He really was from right there in town, but I was oblivious to all of that. I thought I was special because he would come and pick me up and drive me all over town in his Cadillac. I thought, *Okay, he really doesn't have a girlfriend because there's no way he doing all of this and still got someone.* Shit, I thought I was special until one night I was listening to the radio station Midnight Love Dedications. Hell, I heard all the women on the radio saying his name on Midnight Love. Every other dedication was for him. I was like, wait a minute, I thought he was from out of town. All these girls are from in town. I found out through Midnight Love Dedications that he really was from in town, and he had a lot of women. To make things worse, I found out I was pregnant. *How do I tell him this and what will he think?* On one hand I was hoping he would be happy, but I was also thinking, was I really happy about it? The struggle would be real.

I don't know why I thought this Negro would be happy that I was pregnant. When I told him, he became Casper the Ghost and stopped talking to me. He never went to my doctor appointments or checked up on me. He just vanished, and when I went into delivery for my baby, he still was nowhere to be found.

It was a hard pregnancy. I had a few minor complications. I didn't dilate, and they had to induce me three times in order for me to dilate. I ended up having a C-section. I delivered a beautiful baby girl named Drea. She looked just like a little princess, just like a little china doll. Really big cheeks and everything, just the cutest little chubby thing ever.

Even after our daughter was born, he still didn't claim her. After I had my daughter, I went to the one-hour photo to have some pictures taken of her. I started passing them out to friends and family. Well somehow, the pictures started some type of way floating around. It was bad enough that Ray wasn't claiming her, but to add insult to injury, his black ass was living with his girlfriend and she had a baby with him too that he was actually claiming. She was going around saying my baby wasn't his because I was a town hoe, even though she didn't know me. Then I heard she got a hold of the picture and started saying my baby was ugly. Now I know somebody just saying your baby is ugly ain't supposed to trigger you because who cares? But I wanted to fight her anyway, and this was my opportunity.

When all of this happened, I was in junior college. My major was undecided. The only reason why I decided to even attend college was because they were giving away financial aid. Come to find out we both went to the same college. I saw her on that campus. She was short, light-skinned, with shoulder length hair and kinda thick. I had just gotten a fresh weave; my nails had just been done.

I walked up to her. "You said my baby was ugly."

She said, "I sure did!"

I hunched up my shoulders and just stole on her. We fought for what seemed like an hour. I beat the brakes off that girl because I just wanted her to go back beat up to him and let her tell him that it was me. We fought and some of my nails got broken and parts of my weave had loosened. She pulled one of the tracks up. I told her, "It's on! I'm fighting you every time I see your punk ass." I remember calling my hairdresser and saying, "I just fought. I need to come get this weave fixed." We went to the same hairdresser, and I heard she was going to be there the next day. I showed up at that shop and she wouldn't come out of the shop. And I wasn't going to go in because that's where my hairdresser works. I knew she would eventually have to come out the shop. I waited around for about 30-40 minutes, but she wouldn't come out of that shop. I probably should've just let it go, but I was so heated. I wanted to fight her again bad. Don't talk about my daughter! Thinking back, I was mad that his ass was claiming her kid and not mine - the nerve!

My little cousin Hercules and I went to his house to fight her again. We went to the house and were standing in the yard. She had the screen door open. We were going back and forth talking mess to each other. Then she said something about my daughter.

She opened that screen door a little bit more and my little cousin snatched her so fast and landed three blows to her face. They ended up in her house and she was still whooping that girl's ass. We left and I dropped her off at home.

That night, I remember looking out my front window. I thought, *Why is the light messed up?* We had lights around the building and all the lights were out and that had never, ever happened. My mom was over. My newborn was in a bassinet. The bassinet was in my living room, away from the window. My mom was lying on the floor. My twins were sitting on the floor playing or watching TV. I was in the back room, curling my hair.

All of a sudden, I heard a crash and a loud thud. I ran into the living room. Somebody had thrown a brick through my front window, busting the whole front window. It had an M80 attached to it and when it came through the window, it exploded. My baby was okay, because she wasn't close enough. But my twins were all messed up. When the brick exploded on the impact, it embedded pieces into my twins' skin. They had burn marks and brick all over them. My mom was fine. Everybody was scared. I called the police. Then I called Aubrey. He came over right away. He was furious when he saw his kids. The police started telling me that the outside lights were all busted out. The twins had to go to the hospital to get their injuries looked at. I remember watching the doctors at the hospital using some type of tweezer item to dig all the rock out of my kids' skin and they were just crying, but I couldn't help them, which infuriated me.

That night after I took the kids to the hospital, I got my kids back home and put them in the bedroom. My mom went in the room with them. I told her I'd be back. My kids' dad was already out looking for Ray because he knew without a shadow of a doubt it was him. He said he went to Ray's house, but it looked like no one was there. I called all my homegirls. I don't know who the hell we thought we were. We had bats, chains, and all kinds of stuff. We went on The Road to post up.

This bold fucker had the nerve to pull up on the side of us because we parked right in front of one of the stores that was on The Road, and he walked into the store. We were just talking shit with the bats in our hand and shaking the chains. I said, "I know that was you that threw that brick threw my window."

He said, "Bitch, you a damn lie."

I said, "I ought to bust you in the head with this bat. You could have killed my kids, dumb ass."

He said, "I don't know what you are talking about." He got back in his car and drove off.

The girlfriend didn't come to school for about a good week and a half. I don't know if he thought everything had died down or what. But when I saw her again, I beat her ass again. I was defending my child's honor. I didn't care. I was bitter and angry because he wasn't claiming his own child and he hurt my other kids. This Negro had to pay, or someone close to him did. By the time my daughter turned two, I cared less and less if he claimed her. His loss.

One of Ray's cousins hit me up and actually came to see my daughter. My daughter was two by then. The cousin said, "I have nothing to do with the way other people act or whatever the case may be. That's my little cousin, so I want to see her."

I told him, "Okay, you can see her."

He saw her and said, "This Ray's daughter. She looks just like him."

He must've gone and told Ray because all of a sudden, he decided that he wanted to see her. He came back with the cousin. He came in and sat on the couch. My daughter was running around with just a diaper on.

She went up to him and said, "Sing me a song."

He looked puzzled. I thought he was about to belt out Mary Had A Little Lamb, but nah, he started singing TLC's "No Scrubs". The hell kind of nursery rhyme was that? After that, he didn't see her anymore, even though she looked just like him.

It didn't matter because he turned out to be a jail bird. He was always in and out of prison. He ended up having another baby mother besides the one I kept beating the brakes off. She had claimed she wanted his family to know my daughter, so she asked me to bring her over. I brought her over and they said she looked just like one of the aunts who had passed away. His family accepted her, even if he didn't.

CHAPTER 8

Chowchilla Prison

I was starting to get older and I knew I wanted to change my life. I had these children, these four children that I was only receiving welfare for. I needed to figure out a way to make sure I took care of all of them. I started trying to work and find jobs because at this point welfare wasn't enough. I found a bunch of little odds and end type of jobs.

My whole perspective began to change after that scenario. I knew I wanted to better my life, but I wasn't sure how. My name Oya meant warrior, but I was beginning to think that's all it was: a name. I had grown up being an at-risk kid, but I had never worked with at-risk kids. I decided to see about working for a school district.

I got hired with the high school district as campus security. One day while working, these little girls came up to me. They always ran in a pack. I would always see this person picking all of them up. I asked them where they lived. They said they stayed in rooms at group homes. One of them said, "Our group home is hiring."

I said, "What do you need to work there?" Although I had lived in a group home previously, I really didn't know how you work at a group home.

One of the girls gave me the number to the facility. I called up there to find out about the application. The owner's daughter told me to come fill out an application. I filled out that application, but nobody ever called me back. I started calling up there twice a week, leaving a message with the owner's daughter. Erica Grant would tell me her mom wasn't in every single time.

Finally, one day she told me I got an interview with the mom, Linda Grant. I got to the interview. I met with the owners. Her words to me were, "I'll give you a chance, but don't disappoint me." I think she gave me that chance because her daughter told her that she got tired of hearing my voice calling.

That was my first full-time job working at a group home with at-risk youth girls. Shortly after that I met her husband Thomas and their son Thomas Jr. I remember working with these girls and I would bring my kids around the group home girls. They would comb my daughter's hair. We went on trips to the park. We invited some of the group home girls to our birthday parties, because even though it was a business, it was more like a big ole family. I started off as a worker, and about a year later, I was promoted to a facility manager. I shopped for the girls, cooked meals for them, took them to appointments. They were good at times, but when they went off, they would be on one. You have to understand they were in the foster system, and that means they were removed for some reason or another from a caregiver or parent.

Sometimes the girls would be like, "You don't know my life", and I would say, "I know your life all too well because I lived it."

I would take them to their counseling sessions and sit in, not realizing at the time that I needed therapy just as much as they did.

I ended up working for them for five years until they decided to shut down. I was also still working for the school district. I truly appreciated the lessons that I was taught at the group home. One of the things that Mrs. Grant would always say to me was that life was about choices and that I was not responsible for what people did to me. I was only responsible for what I did to people, so choose wisely because my choices will ultimately shape my own outcome.

The Grants were amazing people and my first real job was an eye opener for another facet of at-risk youth. Mrs. Grant has since passed away, but her words truly live on and I have told many people those exact words in my life.

Overall, I really enjoyed working there and I learned a lot about how these kids are pre-judged because they are in a situation that they didn't even ask to be in. I really felt like having that job helped me grow.

I was growing up, but I was still immature because I was still doing dumb shit. During this time there was an incident where I was hanging out a lot and with a particular set of girls. There was another group of girls going around, making it like they were the baddest girl gang in the town. They were just picking on and messing with people and they would try to run random people off the road for no damn reason. They just wanted to be known. They saw me one day at my cousin's house, which was in a Blood neighborhood. They lived on Ninth Street. That's where the Bloods hung out. They saw me and because they didn't like my cousins, I became an immediate target. They were a menace.

I visited my cousins a lot and they saw me there another day getting in my car to leave. They followed me and some of the homies from the street saw them do that, so they got in their car and started following them. We got to the light on Ninth Street and we're like, "What's up? What do you want to do? Because now it's squared up. You ain't going to do shit." They talked a bunch of shit and then they left.

The second time they saw me on this street called Kincaid on the East Side and they were trying to run me off the road as I left, but my friends hopped in their cars and pulled up on me, saying, "Get back to the block." We all met back on Kincaid. They parked further down the street and they started talking a bunch of shit, but they never wanted to fight. They were the talk of the town and would always get out of trouble because they were all juveniles.

One day my cousin and I were going to take the kids to see *The Lion King*. We were at the corner store and happen to be passing by. They were deep in that mini SUV, and they saw my car parked at the corner store. They stopped in the middle of the street and started talking shit again. My cousin started yelling back and forth with them. My cousin ran into the store and said, "They outside." I had recently purchased a .25 for protection. It was so pretty. It had a pink pearl handle and I kept it in my purse. I had two clips loaded in my purse as well. When my cousin came running into the store, all I thought about was protecting my family by any means necessary. My stupid ass took the gun and the clip out and loaded it inside the store where the store owner saw me and I just aimed at them and started shooting. I unloaded both clips on their asses. They started shooting back.

Luckily, no one was hit. There were five kids in that car with us, and no one was hit. They took off there were shell casings all over the ground. Come to find out the police were literally 5.2 seconds away on another call, so when they heard the shots, they came running on foot. My cousin grabbed the gun from me and went across the street, so the police never found the gun. My cousin took all the kids, which were my kids as well, and walked across the street so the kids wouldn't be involved and my kids wouldn't get taken away. I stayed because they knew I was part of it. The store owner told them I had the gun. There was nothing I could do, especially since they found all the shell casings. I was literally caught because it was on the store camera as well.

I ended up giving them the gun. They charged me with a felony. I was literally going to do five years in Chowchilla Prison because of all the charges. The other girls got out that same night because most of them were minors. Their parents came and got them out of juvie. I was in the county for seven months fighting the case. One of the girls from that night ended up in the same cell with me. Come to find out she was on the phone with someone because she had a cell phone snuck in. She was on the phone telling them she was there with the one who was shooting. I was sitting there listening and pissed. We started fighting inside the cell. The guards had to come in and separate us. I was looking at assault as well as the gun charge and shooting a gun in city limits. All I kept thinking about was the stories that my mom told me about every time she got locked up and what she witnessed: women getting curling irons rammed up in their vaginas, brutal fights, just different things like that. I thought there was no way I was going to make it in there. The streets are way different than prison.

Finally, I got a breakthrough when I was told that a witness said they saw the other girls shoot first. I am for certain that was not true because I shot first. I came out of the store shooting, but the witness said they shot first. They believed the witness and they ended up letting me out. I guess it wasn't my time to be in prison. I ended up getting the charges dropped to misdemeanors years later and getting time served because I was in there for seven months. The witness ended up disappearing also. I still say to this day that that witness was my guardian angel because without that testimony, I would have been doing five years in prison. And at the time, my mom was also in Chowchilla, so I would have been in jail with my mom.

I was put on probation for ten years. I couldn't have a gun. After a few years passed, I went and petitioned the court to expunge my record, and they granted it. Almost doing five years in the women's prison had me sit down somewhere quickly.

CHAPTER 9

Looking Back

Although I was trying to grow and become a better person, I reverted back to my old ways. I was raising so many kids. I never really had a man that truly loved me, or that I could call my own. I was partying every so often.

Around this time, I secured a really good job. I thought I was on my way, until one night in 2010. I was attending a party in the downtown area. I was hella tipsy because I hadn't been out in a while. I had gone out with some friends. My homegirl was at the bar and she was talking to a guy, but he seemed like he was interested in me. I was too tipsy to even care if he was or wasn't. I slowly got up from the bar while clenching the chair for support. I got up and started walking towards the bathroom while she was talking to him. I stumbled into the bathroom. The guy ended up following me to the bathroom. He tried to talk to me again while I was by the bathroom.

All I kept saying is, "I just want to go to the bathroom. I just want to go to the bathroom."

He got mad and said, "I am trying to holla at you. Why you acting like this?"

"Acting like what? I do not know you. Get out of here please. I really have to use the bathroom. Please just go."

He said, "Fuck you then, bitch!"

I said, "Who you think you're talking to like that, motherfucker? You don't know me. You better get out of here."

He pushed me into a stall, closed the door, and put his hand over my mouth. He had his elbows pinned on my chest so I couldn't get loose. I tried to push him off of me, but his body weight was too strong for me. I tried to bite his hand, which was covering my mouth, but all that did was piss him off. He took his other hand and slapped me across the face. He said, "If you try to fight me, it's only going to get worse." I felt like I was in slow motion because of the alcohol. He had on a black pea coat. He wasn't an ugly man; he was actually nice-looking. I couldn't really tell his build. He had a short fade haircut. He smelled good. That's really all I remember about him.

To me, it seemed like forever in that bathroom. When he was finished, he ejaculated in me. He pulled up his pants and straightened his pea coat. He said, "Now see, that wasn't so bad." He opened up the stall door and walked out.

I felt so disgusted. I turned my back to the door of the stall and slid down to the floor. I had a skirt on that night. I remember getting the paper towels and I was just cleaning myself. I pulled my skirt back down and I walked out the bathroom door like nothing had happened. I looked around the club to see if I saw him, but he had vanished into thin air. I went to my friend and I told her I was ready to leave - not now, but right now. And we left. I never told a soul, not even her. Probably should have called the police, but to be honest, I just didn't think it would make a difference.

That was on a Saturday night and I had to go to work that Monday. When I got home, I took off the skirt and threw it in the trash. I went into the bathroom and turned on the shower to highest temperature. I didn't get in until I saw steam fogging up the door. I got in and I scrubbed myself what felt like a hundred times. I was just trying to scrub that night off of me. I couldn't understand how a girls' night out turned into me getting raped in the bathroom. So many thoughts just came into my mind. *Why did I keep getting targeted for some many heinous acts? Why does this keep happening to me? Was it my fault because of the way I dressed, because I had on a little skirt? Did I ask for it by getting drunk? Was my response to him too hard, and he was going to pay me back for talking shit?*

I kind of went into a spiral for a while and didn't care about anything yet again. Before the rape occurred, I was in a good place. I had started drinking a little bit, but I wasn't drinking the way I drank in my early years. But now I was drinking a lot. I didn't want a relationship anymore. Everything started coming back. I felt that I was a failure as a parent. I lost a lot of friends because I wasn't communicating or going out. I didn't trust guys at all. I remember when that happened, I was laying in the bed thinking about something Ms. Grant had told me: you're not responsible for what people do to you. You're only responsible for what you do to people. So I had to remember my responsibilities. I had my kids who were dependent on me. They were my responsibility and I couldn't only think of myself in this situation. I made up in my mind that I needed to get it right. Get it together. I told myself that I was going to be better.

By this time, I had gotten my life together. I had a really good job and had gotten a degree. I was thinking to myself, *You can have all the degrees in the world and have this good job. But it doesn't mean anything if you don't value yourself.* And I wasn't valuing myself because of what happened. I needed to change me because everything from the time I was a child up until that point I can't say was my fault. But some of the instances as I got older, I could have made better decisions. My biggest lesson during that time was that I had to learn to teach myself to become better and love me for me. And those were the words that I remembered from her.

I enrolled into a college program, and one of my classes had me focus on ACEs -Adverse Childhood Experiences. When I did research on that, I discovered that there are 10 top ACEs: physical abuse, physical neglect, emotional abuse, emotional neglect, sexual abuse, witnessing domestic violence, substance abuse in the household, mental illness (my mom) in the household, and a family member in jail. I found out that I suffered from nine of the ten but also, in retrospect, actually suffered from all ten. The one that I believed I didn't suffer from was parents divorced or separated. But what I found out in further research is that it can be a parent's separation from the child. So I actually suffered from all ten of them. I learned a lot about myself. It honestly made me reflect on when I was in the group home, when I was in Jamison, all these different things, all the stuff that I lacked, the reason I acted the way I acted. The more ACEs you suffer from, the more your amygdala, your brain, becomes rewired to help you cope with what is happening in your life. So to help you cope, you go from normal daily thoughts to the fright/fight/ flight syndrome. This had basically been my reaction to any event that my brain saw as stressful or dangerous. It also stated that suffering from ACEs activates your nervous system and prepares your body to respond in one of those three ways. I was not scared enough, so I didn't take the fright. I literally don't run from anything, so I didn't take the flight. But I'll fight in a minute. I have had blackouts like when I beat the brakes off of Ray's girlfriend. In my blackouts, people tell me that I look like a different person.

I'm not totally cured. But one way to reverse ACEs is to have caring adults in your life, people who truly care about you, not just somebody who only says they care because they want to have sex, or anything like that. I realized that my high school counselor and my foster parents showed me actual care and concern and did things for me. So I actually had three good people in my life, even though I never knew until my adult years what all of this even was. But now, looking back on everything, I realized and found out things about myself because of ACEs.

I think that counseling is actually what made me start the journey of trying to honestly heal myself, because I've never given myself anything. I tried to make sure everyone is okay around me.

I tried to make sure the kids were okay. I tried to make sure my brother and sister were okay. Anybody that was in my life, I was the protector. I didn't care about what happened to me as long as it wasn't happening to anybody else. When everyone started getting grown and having their own responsibilities, I guess the darkness started coming because I didn't have anything to preoccupy my mind. When I got in my moments when it was just me, a lot of this stuff started coming to the surface that I didn't deal with earlier because I didn't have time to deal with it. I was making sure everyone else was good, which is the way I like it, actually.

ACEs assisted me in rewiring my brain. If it wasn't for the rewiring, I wouldn't be alive today. If it wasn't for the rewiring, I couldn't have walked through fire and walked out polished. If it wasn't for the rewiring, I wouldn't have found resilience. If it wasn't for the rewiring, I wouldn't have found strength.

CHAPTER 10

The Phoenix Rises

I realized that you can't walk around or over your experiences. I had to learn to walk through them because they are the fabric of what builds your character and determination. I was determined not to be like my mom. I was determined not to do my kids the way she did me. I was not going to sell my kids. I was not going to be on drugs. I was not going to have sex with a bunch of men and bring them in and then let my daughter have sex with them. I was determined because of what I went through. I feel like you should never downplay your story, because it's what makes you, you. Tell your story, because you've been through it. You're going to get through it as long as you walk through it. Keep your hands full of you, hold on to you, because at the end of the day, it's only you who will get you through all the fire.

I was told I would never be anything more than a mattress for a man to lay on. I was told that I should be a drug addict to cope, or be a major alcoholic, which I was, kind of. I was told that I should be a prostitute. And sometimes I did have those thoughts in my head. But I'm none of those things.

I hardly cry. I have always felt like crying is a sign of weakness. But I am learning that it's a cleansing, and that's a lesson that I'm still learning. I could say I have a lot to be thankful for because I was also told that some of my experiences happen to women and men alike. But some young kids, they don't make it through it. Some commit suicide, some are prostitutes or dead or in jail, or whatever the case may be. For those who know me, they claim I'm an anomaly. I don't think that. I just feel like it goes back to that determination to not be like my mom.

I have a different relationship with my mom as an adult. I guess that's the one good thing I can say: she taught me determination. I don't remember much else that she taught me. And it was fueled by not being like her. I was going to give my kids everything she didn't give me. I was not going to want my kids to feel like they wanted me dead or wish that I would walk in the middle of the street and get hit by a bus or wish that I would overdose just so we could have a normal life. Those are all the things I wished on her while I was growing up. During those times in my life, if any of those things would have happened, I honestly can't say I would have cared. You know, she wasn't Mama no way, so... I guess that's why I sometimes questioned religion a lot, because why would someone who loves you put you in that situation to be unloved? Why would you send me to her? That's unfair. Why would you give me to somebody who wasn't going to love me?

Even with the odds against me, I beat the odds. I assessed the situation and I went to battle, using my body to protect my fellow man - my brother and sister. I didn't care what happened to me as long as they were safe. Warriors usually protect the kingdom and as long as the kingdom was protected, I was good. My kids call me the matriarch of our family. And to me, a matriarch means that you will go above and beyond yourself and do anything to make sure everyone that is in your tribe is protected.

And that's what I've always done, still to this day. Don't mess with my children, grandchildren, or any close relative of mine. I'm the warrior of my family. I'm going to make sure everybody's okay.

I am a hummingbird. I'm brave, courageous, a fighter, no matter my size. Even as a child, I didn't give up. I stand as beautiful as a lotus flower. I transformed like a butterfly. I rose like a phoenix. I am Lotus, self-regeneration and rebirth. Even when rooted in the dirtiest of water, my trials, the lotus produces a beautiful flower, which is me. I am a butterfly, which signifies rebirth, transformation, change, hope, renewed life, endurance, and the courage to embrace all that comes in your path. I am the phoenix, which signifies transformation, death, rebirth, strength. No matter my trials and my deepest, most horrible times in life. I rose from the ashes to be better and brighter. I survived what I thought should have killed me. I made it through.

Oya comes from Yoruba religion. It means warrior and unbeatable. I am Oya-The Warrior.

POEM

I smile when there is no reason
I smile because I didn't know the woman I'd become in this season
I smile because who knew I'd be birthed a fighter
I smile because every weapon had to retire
I smile because it came to kill me and I killed it
I smile because bitterness was not the effect
I smile because relationships were bad
I smile because I didn't get mad
I smile because they hate me
I smile because I didn't let them break me
I smile because my reflection was tainted
I smile because my reflection now says "I made it"
I smile because I was granted a second chance at life
I smile because "saving grace" was my only device
I continue to smile because "I AM" a "Warrior" that made it to the light.

ABOUT THE AUTHOR

Dess Perkins started from humble beginnings in the streets of Hawthorne CA, where she attended 59th Street Elementary, then relocated to San Francisco, only to end up residing and raising her family in Bakersfield CA. She is the proud mother of five children and currently eight grandchildren. Although life threw many obstacles her way, she persevered through determination and a sheer will not to quit. She went on to work for a prominent group home in Bakersfield and then landed a job with the County of Kern for almost eleven years until she decided to give back and become a teacher. She currently holds a Bachelor's degree in Criminal Justice with a minor in Child Development, a Master's in Business and a Master's in Educational Counseling with a PPS Credential, and currently working on a Master's in Special Education.

Made in the USA
Columbia, SC
27 July 2022